SAINT ELMO'S LIGHT

COLLECTED STORIES OF J THOMAS BROWN

J Thomas Brown

Fenghuang Publishing

Thumb Tacks and Hard Cider are creative nonfiction. The memories of other persons described in those works may be different than the author's. All other stories in this collection are fiction. Any names or characters, businesses or places, events or incidents in the stories are fictitious. Any resemblance to actual persons, living or dead, or actual events in them are purely coincidental.

"Breaking Them with Words" was previously published in Scarlet Leaf Review and Everywhere Stories.

To connect with the author please visit www.jthomasbrown.com

SAINT ELMO'S LIGHT

Contents

Corpus Sancti

Henry, the oldest, had failed to launch. He lived with his family in a house built in 1738 that stood in the middle of twenty acres of corn field in Bucks County, Pennsylvania. George Washington used it as an infirmary for his troops during the Revolutionary War and their blood stains remain in the wide plank floors today. Sometimes, as he fell asleep at night, the worn floorboards, loose on their hobnails, rattled. He would turn the night table lamp on, get up and set the lock on the door latch, then return to bed to wait for sleep with the light on.

The hand-fitted Pennsylvania blue-gray fieldstone walls were two feet thick, but not thick enough to keep out the world's contumely. The airwaves carried in news of the assassination of Dr. King, American war crimes in Vietnam, and the violent 1968 Democratic National Convention protests. Yet life was still pleasant in the old stone house and Henry did nothing to change the world but grow his hair long and sew paisley patches into the legs of his jeans to widen them into bell bottoms.

He dubbed 1968 as The Year of St. Elmo, the patron saint of sailors and those with stomach ailments, whose intestines were wound on a windlass to torture the saint into praying to pagan gods. One sultry evening in early fall he bought a nickel bag of grass from a classmate at a poetry reading by Allen Ginsberg. He returned home afterward and smoked a joint of it in his bedroom. It was so potent the plumed birds on the antique wallpaper came to life and flew around the room. He opened the window to let the smoke out. It was a clammy night with heat lightning flashing. The smell of rain was in the air.

That is when the St. Elmo's Fire came. His sister, Julia, was in the kitchen with a friend. They both saw it and started yelling. An undulating blue light drifted through the screen door and floated into the dining room, gathered itself into a ball and rolled down the hall. At the sound of their shouting, Henry ran down the stairs and into the family room in time to see it pass through the side entrance door. He followed it outside and stood by his car parked at the side of the house. It climbed the copper lightning rod that ran up the stones from the ground up to the rooftop. The fire perched on the spire, hissing. Blue snakes writhed from its rim and a violet glow spread over the roof. The rain gushed at once and plastered his shirt to his skin. He stared until lightning flashed upward from the spire into a cloud overhead and it extinguished.

A week after the visitation of the Corpus Sancti, Henry moved into an apartment in New Hope with a friend. It is said that lightning never strikes twice in the same place, but he knew that was not true.

Awaken - Episode 1: Batsunappen's Dream Portal

The maglev glided in silently to Baltimore at 2:15 p.m. Annie hailed a cab outside the station. "5001 Bayview Boulevard. It's the Hopkins medical annex," she said, sliding into the front seat. When the cab arrived at the medical center, the fare was extracted in netcoin through her cellphone and the pilot drove on to its next fare. Clear Light Sleep Center was listed in the lobby directory as suite 122. She walked with a lopsided gait to the end of the hall.

The waiting room was decorated in soft blue shades. Relaxing Indian dream motifs decorated the walls. Annie signed in, and no sooner had sat down, when Dr. Batsunappen came to greet her. His accent was English with an underlying musical quality.

"I'm Dr. Batsunappen."

She extended a shaking hand. "Annie Taylor."

He was an unusually tall man. His dark complexion contrasted with the starched white coat he was wearing. Annie thought him handsome. It was hard to believe he was a sleep doctor. His manner was lively and brisk.

The doctor escorted his patient down a hallway to his office and motioned her to sit. Statues and paintings from the Indian Vedas and Upanishads adorned the walls and shelves. One wall of the office was filled with shelves of books on sleeping and neurological disorders.

Dr. Batsunappen sat at his desk and studied Annie with curiosity. He noticed her looking at a sculpture set in the wall behind him. "That is called Vishnu Dreaming the Universe." He turned to face the sculpture. "Vishnu is floating on the cosmic ocean, lying on the serpent Ananta. These figures here," he said, gesturing to the upper portion, "represent the five senses. We might wonder in looking at this sculpture, whom is dreaming who."

"Fascinating," said Annie.

"The nature of dreams and reality has always been a central theme in Indian culture. In the Aka-Upanishad, 3,000 years ago, it was written: In dreams, he transcends this world and all forms of death...there are no chariots in that state, no horses, no roads. There are no blessings there, no happiness, no joys, but he himself sends forth blessings, happiness and joys. There are no tanks there, no lakes, no rivers, but he himself sends forth tanks, lakes and rivers. He indeed is the maker."

Annie shook her head. "It's very interesting, but my problem is I haven't slept for three days."

Doctor Batsunappen smiled. "I'm sorry. We must talk about what is troubling you. What's the matter?"

She told him of the pain in her head, the periods of double vision and fatigue, and her inability to sleep. Her features were wan and sunken and her hands shook. Dark circles hung beneath her eyes.

He listened intently and nodded from time to time. "Tell me what you mean when you say, haven't slept. Do you first fall asleep, then wake up, over and over all night? Or are you unable to fall asleep at all?"

"When I begin to fall asleep, this sensation of heat pours over me, and I am filled with pins and needles down my spine and I am wide awake again. It goes on all night. I am so exhausted it hurts." A tear escaped from her right eye and landed on his desk.

He regarded the tear impassively. "You are exhibiting symptoms of severe sleep deprivation and neurological dysfunction. What concerns me is what may be causing it. Some of the symptoms you exhibit are indicative of a problem perhaps in, or near the sleep centers such as the pineal or pons."

Dr. Batsunappen pressed a button built into his desk. "Imaging lab."

A nurse appeared on his screen. "Hello, Dr. Batsunappen."

"I have a Ms. Ann Taylor here who needs a brain scan stat. Can you squeeze her in for an MRI?"

"I see an opening at 3:30. How's that?"

"Thank you. I'll send her over shortly. Before you go, Ms. Taylor, let me show you the sleep lab."

Annie walked with Dr. Batsunappen to a door labelled SLEEP LAB. The doctor ushered her inside. The lab was motel-like in design. Two stories of sleeping rooms lined one side of the cavernous room. "We have one of the largest sleep labs in the country, probably in the world. There are thirty sleeping rooms. Of course, most are empty now, but at night it's full when the real work takes place. Over here we have the monitoring stations: six of them, one for every five patients. They monitor and record all the activity that goes on in the brain and body during sleep."

"I didn't think it would be so large," said Annie.

He led her into one of the chambers. It was like a hotel room, a little smaller and plainer, but completely relaxing. A small night table and chair sat next to a full-sized bed. "Each sleep chamber is very private and comfortable. The conditions for sleep are better than most people have in their own homes. This room is deceiving.

It may appear plain, but concealed overhead in the ceiling, are hundreds of receptors and monitoring sensors. Your body functions and brain waves are picked up by the sensors and sent to the nearest station to be recorded and analyzed."

"I thought there were all kinds of wires you had to hook up," said Annie.

"Not anymore." He opened the night table drawer and produced a small box filled with tiny pink buttons. "We place these 'dimples' on your skin wherever we need to monitor something. You won't notice them at all."

"The sooner I'm in here sleeping, the better," said Annie.

"First we have to scan inside your head and see what's going on." He had a medical assistant take her to Imaging.

After the scan was run and the results recorded, Annie was taken back to the reception room to wait. Dr. Batsunappen, a neurologist by training, remained in Imaging and called in Dr. Mark Payne, a neurosurgeon, to consult.

"I see an abnormality," he said as Dr. Payne squinted through the 3-D scan of Annie's brain.

"Looks like a deep lesion," said Dr. Payne, pointing to a peanut sized spot.

"At the border of the pons. What do you think caused it?"

"It looks like the synapses are burned chemically in the affected area. Perhaps a neurotoxin of some kind escaped the blood brain barrier and the myelin has been damaged. The nerve signals are leaking away to nowhere."

"But how do we fix it?" said Dr. Batsunappen."

"Possibly ablate the scarring with laser surgery, Raji, but it would be risky."

Doctor Batsunappen turned the screen off. "The nerve signals would still be disrupted by the absence of myelin with an ablation.

The weekly grand round is at nine tomorrow morning. We can discuss her case at the meeting."

Annie was still waiting in the reception room when Dr. Batsunappen returned. "We just have to get you set up in the lab. Let's get you checked in," he said, helping her to her feet. A technician helped Annie with her suitcase and led her to a vacant sleeping chamber. She changed into her pajamas, then "dimples" were placed on her temples, at the corners of her eyes, on the sides of her chin, and numerous other places. The technician left and turned out the light.

Despite the comfortable bed and relaxing atmosphere, the cycle of sleep disruption repeated and she did not fall asleep. Annie shuffled her way through the doorway of the monitoring station and stood directly behind the sleep technician. The technician was busy trying to figure out why the recording of her wave patterns on the EEG stopped, when Annie suddenly said: "I can't sleep. Can you give me something?"

The technician jumped in her seat. "God, you scared me to death."

"I didn't mean to. Sorry."

An alarm message popped up on one of the monitor screens.

The technician pushed on a button. "Mike, its Mr. Harrison in room thirty again." She swiveled her chair to face Annie. "He has terrible dreams. They even give me nightmares."

"I didn't know they were contagious," Annie replied, sarcastically.

"I've seen them. Dr. Batsunappen hooks up electrodes to his brain that let you see the dreams, which we record."

"Really? Wow, can I see one?"

The technician shook her head. "Oh no, they're personal information. I can't do that."

"You aren't going to record my dreams, are you?"

She groped for an answer. "That's for the doctor to decide."

"Could I at least have a sleeping pill or a shot or something?"

"The first night we can't give you anything. We have to log your natural patterns first before we try to alter anything. You must go back to your room now. Relax. Sleep comes of its own, when we aren't trying."

As she guided Annie back, cries came through the open door of Mr. Harrison's room. "Mike, close the door for God's sake." A latch clicked into place and the quiet returned.

Annie tossed for hours. Every time sleep started to come, the heat and pins and needles sensation shot through her and brought her back to wakefulness. The pain in her head continued relentlessly.

In the morning, the sleep technician walked in to Annie's room and began removing the sensors. "You didn't sleep at all. I could tell from the graphs."

Annie gulped down the water on the night table. "Brilliant."

"You can have a shower and get some breakfast in the cafeteria, then you'll feel better."

Annie dropped down heavily in the chair in front of the doctor's desk. "What did the tests show doctor? Am I fixable?"

"Let me go over what we've found and what the options are for you," said Dr. Batsunappen. "The scan showed a lesion near the area of the brain that regulates the circadian rhythms. We call your condition an intrinsic dyssomnia."

"You're over my head already."

"There is damage to an area of your brain that regulates sleep. The damaged area tried to heal itself and formed a lesion, or scar, over the affected brain tissue. That's why you're unable to remain asleep; the scar tissue can't conduct the nerve impulses. The impulses to the sleep center are leaking away or distorted"

Her shoulders heaved and she wiped away the tears falling from her right eye and down her cheek. "I'm crying from just one eye. I'm so screwed up."

He patted her hand. "We discussed your condition at a meeting of the university neurologists this morning. Normally this kind of condition can't be corrected, that is – not until now. One of the team members talked about something new that has just been developed. It has worked in preliminary tests. It's called RMC. Recombinant metal crystallography. It's a kind of liquid metal that can be directed to the damaged area through the cerebral veins where we weren't able to get to before, and then be activated to bypass the scar tissue and restore the nerve impulses."

Annie pulled her hand away. "I can't believe this is happening to me and what you're telling me. I'll be an experiment."

Dr. Batsunappen looked her in the eye. "It would be much less intrusive than conventional brain surgery. A much faster recovery is expected. The operation would only take an hour, and in a day or so, you would be right as rain. But this is a big decision and you need time to think about it."

"That's not necessary. There doesn't seem to be any other choice."

"Good, I'll make the arrangements," said Dr. Batsunappen, reassuringly. "We'll get you transferred from the sleep clinic to the hospital medical center and get you a room over there. You'll be given a sedative prior to the surgery, then brought to the OR. There is no need to be put under for this procedure. The brain has no feeling or ability to sense pain in itself, so you'll receive a local anesthetic."

He pressed the com button. "Admissions, please."

An office administrator appeared on the screen.

"This is Dr. Batsunappen. I need to admit a new patient, Ms. Ann Taylor. Send an aide over, please."

An orderly helped Annie into a wheelchair. It was a long way to her room in the neurological wing. A nurse followed them in and helped Annie change into a hospital gown and climb into bed.

"The operation's at 1:00," said the nurse.

"Can I make some calls?" asked Annie.

"You sure can." The nurse pressed on the side of the bedside table and a com panel popped up. Annie keyed in her mother's number.

"We're coming to see you," said her mother after she was told the troubling news.

"You don't have to. They're taking good care of me. The operation is this afternoon and they say I'll be out of here by tomorrow."

"You're going to need at least a day or two to get back on your feet. Your father and I want to help out, so it's not an option. We'll get the next flight to Baltimore and be there tomorrow afternoon."

The nurse returned, pushing a cart containing two syringes. "Okay Annie. The anesthesiologist will be here in a second to get you ready. We're going to give you a few shots and get you numb."

"We love you. Think positive thoughts," her mother said.

"I love you, too." She disconnected.

The anesthesiologist was a wiry man with sunken cheeks and an intense expression. "We're taking all the precautions we can to insure there's no discomfort. The brain has no ability to feel pain itself, so you won't feel anything. We're going to introduce the liquid metal device through an incision in your cranium, then the surgeon will guide it to the lesion using a magnetic system. Do you have any questions you'd like to ask me?"

Annie shook her head. "I can't think of any."

"Okay. I'll get started then. I'm going to give you a local anesthetic in your scalp and a sedative that will allow you to be conscious enough to respond to any questions." He gave Annie an injection in the arm. A pleasant warmth began spreading throughout her body.

The nurse started shaving Annie's hair and Annie smiled, laughing as tufts of it fell about her. "You're cutting off my hair, aren't you?"

"We have to honey," replied the nurse.

When her head was denuded, the anesthesiologist picked up a second syringe and began making quick injections in a circle on the top of Annie's head.

"Feel this?" he asked, scratching her head with his fingers.

Annie looked up quizzically. "Feel what?"

A ubiquitous light with no apparent source filled the Spartan operating room. A nurse and an aide wheeled in Annie and lifted her onto the operating table that sprouted from the middle of the floor like a lotus pad. The anesthesiologist inserted a small shunt into the back of Annie's hand, then pulled a tube from the side of the lotus and attached it to the shunt. Annie watched with curiosity as a clear liquid filled the tube and entered her body.

Two suited physicians entered the OR tugging at their surgical gloves. Despite the surgical dress, hair cap and mask, she recognized the tall frame of Dr. Batsunappen. "I guess this is it, Dr. Batsunappen."

"You're doing just fine. This is Dr. Payne, who will be performing the surgery."

Annie didn't know him and couldn't make out his face. She tried to speak, but the combination of her exhaustion and the sedative made the choosing of words difficult, and it was hard to focus through the mental haze. "Tell him to go," she said drunkenly.

Dr. Payne peered down at Annie and laughed. "Could I have some of what she's having? That's how I want to feel."

She tried to sit up, but her body wouldn't respond. The paralyzing effect of the drugs had taken hold.

Dr. Batsunappen held Annie's hand. "Sometimes there's a brief panic reaction to the sedative. It will only last a moment. Believe me, you're in the best of hands. Dr. Payne is an outstanding neurosurgeon."

"Soon you'll feel like a new person and be sleeping like a baby again," added Dr. Payne. He nodded to the anesthesiologist.

Annie felt the warmth returning, but this time stronger and with a sense of detachment that was so great, she didn't care about anything. He wheeled over a laser scalpel that the surgical staff had nicknamed "Gort," and activated a series of metallic curved rods that emerged from the surface of the operating table in a ring about Annie's head. When she was completely encircled and locked into position, display panels in the wall of the operating room sprang to life, revealing the contents inside her head in minute detail, along with graphs of vital statistics.

Dr. Batsunappen studied the information, then marked her scalp with a skin dye to indicate the point of entry. Dr. Payne trained Gort on the speck of dye and an almond shaped lid opened on the front. A greenish beam, so thin it was barely visible, emerged from the eye-like aperture. It grew in length and met with Annie's scalp, then went deeper into her skull. There was a momentary sizzle, then it extinguished, disappearing back into Gort's eye. The lid closed silently.

Dr. Payne pushed the laser away impatiently and picked up a syringe containing the recombinant liquid metal. Watching the display of Annie's skull intently, he inserted the needle into the hole made by the laser beam.

"You're right over the fissure, just a little deeper," said Dr. Batsunappen. "Right there."

"I'm beginning the injection," replied Dr. Payne. He clamped the syringe in place and activated the plunger. The programmable liquid resembled mercury in appearance as it flowed silently downward through the needle and into the brain. As it flowed through the complex network of veins, it blipped its location on a display panel. With guidance from both doctors, it arrived at a point beside the pons. It had taken about thirty minutes to reach its destination. The integration of the liquid metal with the living native brain tissue was the most dangerous part of the operation, but would only take seconds.

Dr. Batsunappen stood beside her at the operating table and observed her demeanor. "Ms. Taylor, can you hear me?"

She responded from far away. "Yes."

"We're ready to activate the device now. Are you comfortable?"

"There's no pain."

"You may feel yourself falling asleep suddenly, but that's nothing to worry about. Try to relax, don't fight it." He nodded to Dr. Payne, who removed the syringe from the hole in her skull.

Dr. Batsunappen keyed in a series of program commands at the control panel on the wall. A few seconds later, PROGRAM COMPLETE displayed. Annie's eyes widened in surprise, then closed as smoothly as Gort's lid. He studied the display for a several minutes, then announced: "She's entering phase two and going deeper. She's sleeping."

The medical crew congratulated one another with smiles and backslaps, ringing Annie as she slept on the lotus petal.

The next morning, Dr. Batsunappan observed the output from Annie's brain, worried she was not leaving REM sleep. The sleep lab monitors showed her to be submerged in the deepest level of the dreaming states. The sensors around her eyes picked up continuous rapid eye movement, sometimes exaggerated and frantic.

He at first thought it was natural to sleep so long because she had a four-day sleep deficit to make up. She had been in deep rapid eye movement sleep, the deepest stage four dreaming phase, since the liquid metal device had been activated. Typically that deepest state of sleep would last about fifty-five minutes, then the sleeper would recycle back through the previous stages before re-entering stage four REM again. After three or four iterations of cycling, the sleeper would awaken fully.

A medical aide entered the monitoring station and informed Dr. Batsunappan Annie's parents were in the waiting room. "I'll be right there," he said.

The doctor spotted a nervous looking middle-aged couple sitting near the entrance and shook hands with both parents, smiling confidently. "I'm Dr. Batsuappan. Let me take you to her room and I'll explain on the way. It's a bit of a walk, I'm afraid."

"Is this part of the hospital?" her mother asked.

"The sleep center is an adjunct of Hopkins. Your daughter is here because the portion of her brain that controls sleep was damaged and we are the best equipped to deal with her problem."

"How is she? We were told the operation went well," her father said.

"It did." Dr. Batsunappan quickly summed up the preceding events leading to her arrival after the operation. "She's still sleeping," he explained as they neared her room.

They stopped outside the door. "She said she would be coming home today," said her mother. "Is everything all right?"

This was the part he hated. There were irregularities that he couldn't possibly explain to laymen, even if he did have the answers. Summoning up his will power, he put on his best poker face, opened the door and gestured them to enter. "We expect a full recovery." He had almost dared to hope to find her awake, but the sleep was still profound, and it seemed there was no one inhabiting her body. The mystery of consciousness loomed unsolved before him. "I'll leave you with her."

After her parents sat by the bedside watching her for half an hour, her father picked up her hand. "Annie, we're here." There was no response.

An hour went by and a nurse came in with a cart. "I need to check a few things. We only let people stay for an hour after surgery," she said, tugging on the privacy curtains.

Her mother kissed her on the forehead. "We love you, Annie," she said as they rose to go.

Dr. Payne joined Dr. Batsunappan in the monitoring room the following morning. "How is she?"

Usually, a change occurs in chemical and electrical activity in the central nervous system that releases the sleeper from the paralysis of sleep, but Annie's was missing. The sleep doctor nervously tapped on the display. "There's another piece to the puzzle we don't understand yet. She's exhibiting continuous rapid eye movement, sometimes frantic. That indicates nightmares."

"What are you saying?"

Dr. Batsunappen regarded his colleague sadly. "She is unable to awaken."

Dr. Payne bit his lip. "I never would have imagined this happening. We'll have to develop some sort of reverse procedure to undo everything. God knows how long that will take."

"Come with me," said Dr. Batsunappen. His colleague had difficulty keeping up. They walked to the far end of the hall to the last room. A man lay on his back, pallid and sunken. A bundle of wires ran from the top of his shaven head to a small black box. The box was the size of a box of tissues; black and smooth with one on-off switch and one jack with a plug that contained the cable that was wired into the patient's skull. On the wall hung a large display panel. The patient appeared to be asleep, although his breathing was weak and irregular.

"This is John Harrison," said Dr. Batsunappen. "He was diagnosed with advanced cancer when he was brought here five years ago. He has neither insurance nor financial assistance, so he has volunteered to help us in our research."

"What research?"

Dr. Batsunappan studied his colleague carefully. "Dream research. His cancer produced psychological trauma – fear of dying – and a disturbed sleep filled with nightmares about dying. Because of the research conducted here, I've been able to develop a tool to aid with healing sleep disorders. It's a dream portal."

"Dream portal?" His eyes darted nervously back and forth over the neurologist's face.

"Students of neurology are taught our brains are compartmentalized and mapped, that each part has a specific function, and that the billions of memory cells contain specific memories hard-coded to certain locations. We're taught it's impossible to understand the great complexity of this organ."

Dr. Payne resented being patronized. "Yes, yes. That's what we all learned in medical school."

The sleep doctor patted his colleague's arm reassuringly. "Put all that away now. The brain is not hard-coded at all. It's an open-ended receiver and transmitter that is based on electrical signals. I'm able to read the electrical signals generated during sleep and direct the output to a display screen. I can convert the signals to real time imagery so that we can see a live dream as it happens. They can be recorded and played back to regenerate the dream."

Dr. Payne shook his head in disbelief.

"I know it's asking a lot for you to accept this idea, but I'll show you it's true."

Dr. Batsunappen plugged an output from the box which was connected to Mr. Harrison to the display screen. Images began to form, then voices were discernible. The outlines sharpened until the dream began to congeal. The images were at first eidetic and cartoonish, then became smoother in motion and more realistic in color. It was a remarkable likeness and played like a movie on the screen.

John Harrison stood in a large garden shed with a dozen people who were younger than himself. They milled about the over-crowded shed aimlessly until the door suddenly burst outward. He and the others fell out of the shed and into a lake. They swam out to a motorboat and began climbing over the sides into the boat, then the boat began to sink. The patient began thrashing in the water as the dream continued playing on the screen.

"It doesn't make much sense to us, but it is important to him," said Dr. Batsunappen.

"It's like a portal to another world," said Dr. Payne in astonishment.

"I'll hook up Ann Williams and use it to communicate with her. There is a way to control her nightmares. Will you help me?"

"We should discuss this at the round table first."

Dr. Batsunappen frowned, shaking his head. "We have to act now."

Both doctors worked quickly to disconnect Mr. Harrison from the dream portal and placed the equipment on a cart, wheeling it over to Annie's room. Dr. Payne ordered a local anesthetic to be brought in. He administered several injections around the incision made by Gort. Carefully cutting away the freshly healed skin over the opening, he inserted the wire lead from the dream portal into the hole in the bone that was now exposed.

Dr. Batsunappen turned on the dream portal. "Isn't it ironic that we are looking today into the land of dreams, the place of magic and prophecy for thousands of years – with science?" As her eyes darted frantically beneath her eyelids, the screen began to brighten. Images began to form, then sharpen and deepen in color.

The doctors watched intently. The dream was seen through the camera of Annie's mind's eye. The camera swooped down on massive iron gates at the front entrance of a great estate. A private road bordered by brooding pines ran through an expanse of lawn to a large greystone house at the far end. The landscape was locked in the grip of winter. The camera took them inside the house, where Annie and her parents congregated in one of the rooms.

She looked out through a window onto the lawn as billowing clouds poured over the horizon. They quickly covered the estate and overshadowed the house, darkening the interior.

"We have to go right now," shouted Annie. All three occupants ran out of the house and across the lawn, Annie in the lead. She led them down the driveway toward the iron gates. Before they reached them, the gates swung open and admitted three black hearses that streaked down the road and headed for the house. They generated a whooshing noise as they cut through the air. The hearses stopped in unison, their back hatches swinging open to emptiness, demanding passengers.

"Run," shouted Annie. As she ran across the lawn it became evident her legs were becoming weaker with each stride. She slowed to a lopsided gait, struggling to continue. Then she saw the pit, a moss lined hole in the earth the size of a swimming pool. Something was moving down in the pit.

The physicians watched the graphs measure her fear in terms of heartbeat and respiration and hormonal levels. "These are her underlying psychological processes," said Dr. Payne. "They need to play themselves out. She'll find resolution in her own way."

"Look at the output, she's under great stress. It's real to her. We got her into this," said Dr. Batsunappen, angrily.

They watched as her fear drew her like a magnet to within three feet of the edge of the pit. She spoke to whatever was lurking in the hole: "Show yourself. I know you're there. I'm not afraid of you."

A form began to rise over the side. As it slowly climbed and began to materialize, the stress graphs pegged all the way, belying her words. The face was that of a gaunt and emaciated creature whose sallow skin was nearly rotten. The dark hollows of its eyes spoke disease. The figure stood, towering over Annie. It lifted a long-sleeved arm, the cloth of its coat falling back to expose a fleshless hand. The face leered, the hand extended, and Annie put out her own in self-defense. The thing was stronger than she was. When her hand met its fleshless bones, it began to push her into the earth with a supernatural force. The mossy ground parted about her useless legs and began to swallow her up. "Someone help – help me please," she pleaded.

"Do no harm," said Dr. Batsunappen, unable to break away from the scene on the display panel.

"We should not interfere."

"If you're thinking it doesn't matter because it's only a dream, you're full of crap."

Dr. Payne looked down at Annie on the bed. Her lips were moving. Inarticulate moans escaped. "She's your patient, Raji. What do you want to do?"

"We can help her take control of her dreams, at least ease her through this until we come up with the cure. I'll teach her to use a Tibetan technique called clear light dreaming."

"She's asleep, damn it! How the hell are you going to teach her anything?" He sneered at his colleague contemptuously, convinced of his insanity.

Dr. Batsunappan picked up the lead to the display panel and thrust it at Dr. Payne. "Hook it up to the audio-video," he ordered.

The neurosurgeon stepped sideways and reached for the red emergency button instead.

"Don't. Trust me. Hook it up, please, Mark."

Dr. Payne clenched his teeth and plugged in the cable. Dr. Batsunappen plugged the other end into the jack on the dream portal, then keyed commands into the system. He stepped back a few feet to place his entire body in view of the built-in camera lens of the display.

The image of Dr. Batsunappen appeared in the dreamscape standing next to Annie in full view of the phantasm. He moved to one side so that Annie could see him better. The phantasm lifted its bony hand from Annie's and stared silently at the doctor who had entered through the dream portal. The physician appeared like a glowing angel of mercy against the cold barrenness of Annie's dreamscape.

"Help me doctor. Get me out of here, please," sobbed Annie.

The doctor tried with difficulty to control his emotions. "Ms. Taylor, the operation wasn't a success. We're still working on the cure. We need to show you a way to deal with this until we can make the right adjustments."

"Can't you get me out of here, can't you help me?"

The creature advanced to Annie and began pushing her back into the ground.

"Ignore that thing," said Dr. Batsunappen. "It's a part of you. It can't hurt you."

"How can I – it won't let me go."

"I know it seems hard, but if you use your will, it is possible. You can take control of this dream. You'll have to do exactly as I tell you. Once you know how, you can make your own dreams – you can be The Maker. Remember the verse I told you? 'In dreams, he transcends this world and all forms of death...he himself sends forth blessings, happiness and joys. He is The Maker.'"

"I remember."

"Repeat these words with all your will power, with all your intent. Don't hesitate in your conviction: I will awaken within the dream and know that I am dreaming."

Annie looked into Dr. Batsunappen's wild shining eyes, repeating the words.

"Say it again."

She continued looking into his eyes, repeating it a second and a third time.

"Good. Hold out your hands in front of you. Look down at them and watch them closely." Annie held out her hands and looked down. "Do you understand that they are your hands in your dream?"

"I do," she replied.

"Now turn them over slowly so your palms are face up."

Annie obeyed. The creature stepped back and watched through its sunken eye sockets.

"Do you understand that you have moved your hands in your dream with your own will?" She nodded. "Yes, I moved them with my will." "Now, look down at your legs. Do you understand that they are your legs in your dream?" She nodded again. "I understand." "Then use your will to lift them out of the soil. They're your legs and subject to your will."

Annie pulled her right leg upward. The soil formed a suction that resisted her efforts, but the leg slowly lifted, an inch at a time, until her entire leg was free. She began working on her other leg, repeating the process until she stood with both feet on the mucky soil. Her lips trembled and tears ran down her cheeks.

"The rest is up to you. You must make your own way through your world now. You are The Maker." He nodded to his colleague.

"Bravo, Raji," said Dr. Payne, disconnecting the plug.

Annie stared at the empty space where Dr. Batsunappen had been. She turned to face the phantasm. It leered into her face, waiting to see what she would do. She forced her legs into motion and began running, slipping and falling at first, then gaining speed, leaving the pit behind.

She climbed a stone wall and ran into thick woods. The presence of the thing was behind her as she pushed through saplings and thorns to escape it. When she came to Silver Lake, where she had skated as a girl, the primordial presence stopped at the shoreline. She glided onto the ice and willed skates on her feet, and with a sideways shove of her leg, pushed her weight into motion. It became night and the moon reflected across the frozen surface in a shimmering streak of blueish moonbeams. Under the moon, her graceful form danced in harmony with the night, her happiness deepening as she leapt into the air spinning and free.

Awaken - Episode 2: Free Will

There was a knock on the door. A nurse leaned halfway into the room. "Ann Taylor's parents are here. Should I tell them to come back at eleven?"

Dr. Batsunappan rubbed his forehead to erase from his mind the image of the phantasm in his patient's nightmare. He glanced at his watch. "Show them to my office."

Dr. Payne waited for the door to close. "What did I just see a few minutes ago? Am I to believe you were communicating directly with the mind of a human being, or was that some sort of prerecorded hoax?"

"It was no stunt, Mark." Dr. Batsunappan looked down at Annie sleeping on the bed. "We are at the cusp of something much larger than ourselves. Consciousness never sleeps. It is always at work. During the day, it guides us through the world to ensure our physical survival. In our sleep, it is assembling the events and experiences of our waking world into the personality that we call the self. The inner world becomes the outer world. My portal is a machine that can pierce through the organic barrier called the brain into the electricity of the self-aware mind. Consciousness is electrical. I've only mastered some of the lower frequencies of the sleeping stages. There is little doubt that soon we will be able to communicate at all stages of consciousness, including the wakeful states."

Dr. Payne dragged a chair to Annie's bedside and slumped down beside her. "I never thought of it that way. It's just that it hasn't sunk in completely. But I've gone from total cynic to … maybe. This might be the greatest breakthrough in medical technology in a hundred years."

Dr. Batsunappan patted his colleague on the back. "My paper is coming out in the *Journal of Neurology* next month. I need all the backing I can get."

Dr. Payne looked up. "For now, we have to find out what went wrong with the operation."

"I need a team on this. I'll bring in the whole department if I have to."

"That means Gottlieb, too."

Dr. Batsunappan turned to go. "Even old Gottlieb. Thanks for your help. I do need your support. Excuse me, the Taylors are waiting."

The Taylors' patience was stretching thin. He could feel the tension in the air as he sat down at his desk. "I apologize for making you wait. I know how stressful this is for you."

"Why can't we see her?" asked her father.

"Visiting hours are usually eleven to eight. Your daughter has not awakened yet and we are still conducting tests to check on her condition this morning."

"Condition?" said her mother. "What condition?"

Dr. Batsunappan shifted back in his seat. "Mrs. Taylor, let me start over. Although it is unusual to sleep so long after brain surgery, this is not the first time it has happened. The term condition can refer to any state of well-being. Her vital signs are good, but she has not yet awakened."

"It's after eleven now. Can we see her?" her father asked.

The doctor cringed of the thought of their parental reaction to seeing her wired into the dream portal. "We're still running the tests. Come back this evening."

The Taylors grunted their consent and rose to leave. "Wait a minute," said Dr. Batsunappan. "It's good that you're here. I don't see her occupation mentioned in her medical history. We need to look into possible causes of the lesion. What does she do for a living?"

"She's a stock broker," said Mrs. Taylor.

He keyed the information into his computer. "Any hobbies? Pastimes?"

"She loved to ice skate, but when she was training for the national championship she broke her ankle and it never healed the same." Mrs. Taylor glanced at her husband.

He smiled. "She likes to work on her sports car."

"I'm sorry to hear about the ankle," said Dr. Batsunappan, "skating for the championships takes a lot of talent." He chuckled as he typed. "Sports car. That's cool."

After the Taylors left, he contacted Brenton Biotronics, the company that had written the software for the liquid metal device. They agreed to send a senior programmer in the morning to examine the procedure that was used on Annie and to find a way to reprogram the device if necessary. Dr. Batsunappan informed several of his colleagues in the neurology department of what had happened and asked them to come and observe his patient first hand. The small audience, including the programmer, was to assemble at nine the following morning in the monitoring station.

He worked on updating Annie's progress notes and the records of his other patients. Later that afternoon, he and Annie's nurse put the dream portal in a closet, then swaddled her head so that the wires were hidden. He instructed the nurse to let the Taylors visit until eight o'clock, then left for the day.

Dr. Batsunappan arrived at the sleep center a half hour early the next morning to reconnect the dream portal, then went to the monitoring station. While waiting for the team to assemble, he checked over Annie's readouts. During his twenty years as a neurologist, he had on rare occasions witnessed the impossible, and he had not given up hoping for just one more miracle. One patient of his had meningitis caused by e coli bacteria. The bacteria had destroyed all the neocortex and the man was declared brain dead. The prognosis was five years or less on life support as a vegetable. On the fifth day of the vegetative state, the family met at the patient's bedside to discuss disconnecting life support. Suddenly his eyes opened and he called out: "I'm still here." A month later he was fully recovered.

Dr. Batsunappan was frowning over her EEG when the others arrived: Dr. George Gottlieb, head of neurology; Dr. Carol Lyons, a neuropsychiatrist, Dr. Payne, and Dr. Laticia Green, a senior programmer from Brenton Biotronics.

"Well, doctor, what do you have for us?" asked Dr. Gottlieb. He stood beside Dr. Batsunappan and began to scrutinize the readout on the screen.

Startled, Dr. Batsunappan turned to face them.

"Dr. Latricia Green, from Brenton. I'm not a medical doctor," said the programmer, sticking out her hand. "PhD in biomedical programming. Call me Latrice."

Dr. Batsunappan pumped her arm vigorously. "Thank you for coming on such short notice, Latrice. Hello Dr. Lyons."

"I got your memo, but I still don't have a clear idea yet what's going on."

Dr. Batsunappan went over the medical history in detail, hoping Latrice could keep up, then turned to Dr. Gottlieb. "You'll notice on the readout, Doctor, there has been no change for more than two days."

The older physician shook his head. "Never saw anything like it before. The wave patterns indicate continuous REM 4: paradoxical sleep."

"This is certainly not a coma," said Dr. Lyons. "Accelerated heartbeat and respiration. Constant synchronized eye movement. She's dreaming her ass off."

Dr. Batsunappan smiled wryly. "Would you like to see what's going on inside her head right now?" He watched the expression on everyone's face with amusement.

"He's not joking," said Dr. Payne.

They followed Dr. Batsunappan down the hall to Annie's room. She lay on the bed breathing heavily, sometimes mumbling unintelligibly. "This is Ann Taylor," he said.

Dr. Gottlieb bent down level with the dream portal and eyed it closely. "Is this it: the neuro-communicator?"

"I call it a neuro-translator, but that's it," said Dr. Batsunappan.

"Show us."

Dr. Batsunappan had set up for the demonstration in advance. The neurologists and programmer stood at the foot of the bed and regarded the screen over the headboard. He switched it on.

It was twilight in the dead of winter and Annie was skating on Silver Lake. Gaining speed, she turned backward and pirouetted into the air. As she spun, her body dissolved and flickered into nothingness. The scene changed and she was hovering in the air over an empty stretch of country highway. An antique sports car purred down the concrete road with the top down and two people inside. The conscious being with no body that was Annie followed behind the car for several moments, then connected. She became the passenger, but her dream sheath was her high school self. She looked at the driver. It was Dennis Ropeson, her high school boyfriend. It was nearly dark and they were in a mystery sports car rally, driving in an old MGA convertible that smelled oily and rattled on the hard pavement. They were lost on the back roads, surrounded by open expanses of rolling farmland.

She was the navigator, reading from a list of clues in the form of riddles that determined the route of the race. "Turn west of the water tower, then prepare to get a shower."

"Do you see a water tower?" asked Dennis.

"Not really."

"Let's pull over and look at the map."

She shrugged. "Okay."

Dennis pulled to the shoulder, but instead of taking out a map, he produced a blanket and proceeded to spread it on the ground by the side of the road. "I think we ought to sit on the blanket and look at the map."

"Dennis, you don't have a map," said Annie.

"It's in the trunk."

She sat down beside him anyway. Dennis put his arms around her and gave her a slow kiss, which she returned. Suddenly a meteor streaked over the horizon and ended in a flash of brilliant sparkling light.

"Wow, what was that?" asked Annie.

"A meteor."

Two more shot over the horizon trailing long ribbons of bright light that illuminated the twilight.

"Wow!" they said in unison.

Hundreds of meteors began pouring through the sky and Annie's heart rate skyrocketed. The two teenagers watched in awe. The meteors emanated a message from the voids of space: the answer is here, the quest is won, the numina of existence have come. The dazzling streaks of luminosity were messages of enlightenment, promising all the answers the human race sought since the beginning of the great whatever.

Dennis leapt up and ran across the road to the field where the meteors appeared to hit. Annie ran after him, close at his heels.

"Wow, wow!" they shouted together.

The meteors began a transmutation into flying alien spacecraft, becoming giant globes of pulsating luminosity humming with energy. One hovered over Dennis and pulsed vibrantly, encircling him in rings of light. He ascended slowly toward the globe inside the rings, writhing in ecstasy. "Annie, Annie. They know it all. Come join them, it's wonderful."

Annie was encircled by the rings of light and began ascending to the globe hovering above her. She felt peace and harmony in the light. The light promised the answers she longed for. She could join and be one with them; to just let go and know the *why* of everything; to enjoy eternal contentment and complete knowledge. She wanted to let go. But something held her back.

"Don't. Dennis, don't. You won't be you anymore. You'll lose your free will."

Dennis disappeared through the iris-like opening in the belly of the craft and was gone. As soon as Annie understood what the globes wanted, they rejected her, and she began falling. She hit the earth and rolled, then ran, trying to escape as they swooped down on her like angry birds.

A hot burst of light hit a rock nearby and it exploded. She zigzagged across the field, narrowly escaping several more, which showered her with debris.

Annie stopped and looked at her hands, turning the palms upward. *These are my hands in my dream, and subject to my will.* She closed her eyes and breathed deeply. Gathering all her will power, she said aloud: "Pull out."

The screen went blank. "What the hell?" said Gottlieb. After several moments a gray static appeared, then coalesced into the image of Annie spinning back down to the surface of Silver Lake. She smiled happily at her audience and did a triple Lutze in the moonlight.

Dr. Batsunappan switched off the portal and faced the team of experts, expecting cheers or an ovation. They remained staring at the blank screen in silent astonishment. "Any questions or comments?" he asked.

"The lake must be a sort of safety mechanism for her. A place where she feels safe," said Dr. Lyons. "That was very personal and private. I felt like – a voyeur."

"It's a milestone," said Dr. Payne. "It has applications far beyond medical use."

Dr. Gottlieb snorted condescendingly. "It's very impressive, but it's not going to save this patient. I want you all to meet me in the conference room. Dr. Batsunappan, you do what you need to do to get her disconnected, then join us."

Awaken - Episode 3:
Dreams of Dreams

D r. Gottlieb held up his hand for silence. "Does anyone else have reservations about what they just witnessed in there, or am I the only one? Dr. Lyons, I think I detected a note of concern on your part. You said you felt like a voyeur."

Dr. Lyons looked at the white-haired physician inquisitively. "This neuro-translator development could revolutionize psychiatry. It's amazing. A blessing, if we can believe everything we just saw. But on the other hand, it's like spying on someone's mind. We have to be careful."

"Raji is going to release his paper to the *Journal of Neurology* in a few weeks," said Dr. Payne. "More testing needs to be done, and when scientifically verified, we can proceed to the ethical considerations. There will have to be new rules, I'm sure."

Gottlieb hunched forward. "Who here has looked at Ms. Taylor's medical chart?"

"I did," said Dr. Payne. "Before and after the round table to operate on her lesion. It's SOP."

"Was there a consent signature for the neuro-communicator procedure?"

Dr. Payne stared blankly and chewed the inside of his cheek. "For the neuro-*translator*? No. I didn't see one."

Gottlieb paused dramatically. "There is no patient consent form to perform the operation."

"I clearly remember her signature approving the experimental use of recombinant liquid metal for her lesion. Can't it be considered as an extension?"

Dr. Batsunappan appeared in the doorway. Dr. Gottlieb pointed to an empty seat. The smile on the dream doctor's face quickly faded. He had hoped for a more enthusiastic greeting.

"Dr. Batsunappan, can you explain why there isn't a consent signature for Ann Taylor's neuro-communicator procedure? Which by the way, hasn't been approved for testing yet."

He straightened in his seat and smiled incredulously at Gottlieb. "Of course. She was unconscious."

"There was an entry made the next day into the family history record after you interviewed her parents. Why didn't you obtain *their* consent as next of kin?"

Dr. Batsunappan looked around the table and rested on Dr. Lyon's face imploringly. He had hoped for her backing more than anyone else's.

She shook her head disapprovingly. "It's a privacy violation without consent, Raji."

"Dr. Batsunappan," said Gottlieb, "I am taking this matter to the medical ethics board immediately. I suggest you don't practice medicine until we have a decision from them. Are there more violations of other patients we need to worry about?"

"You can't do this. Because of the paperwork? What about my patients?"

Gottlieb shook his finger in Raji's face. "You think not? What about your patients? They need protection from half-baked idiots like you. That's why there are rules."

"What about Annie Taylor?"

"You and Dr. Payne will share your records and notes with Latrice so she may reprogram the implant. Is that okay with you, Latrice?"

Latrice coughed, then forced a strained smile. "Of course, doctor. But this isn't going to be simple. I'll need the transcripts of the operation and the subsequent patient data. Now that I know the extent of the problem, I'll need to share the data with two of my programmers..."

Gottlieb frowned at Dr. Batsunappan and turned to Dr. Payne. "You see that the HIPAA requirements are taken care of so they can have access to the patient records."

Dr. Payne nodded.

The senior physician pushed himself away from the table and rose. "Okay. Let's get going."

Dr. Batsunappan walked back to the dream lab alone. He didn't hear the receptionist's greeting when he went by. He slumped down in his seat and swiveled around to face the sculpture of Vishnu Dreaming the Universe. The dream portal was the culmination of years of work. If the journal accepted the science behind it, he would receive wide recognition and acclaim. There could be grants. Clear Light Technologies would explode onto the stock market. If it didn't topple instead. The meeting played like a bad movie inside his head. He hadn't seen it coming; it was too surreal not to be real.

He swung back to his desk and called the receptionist. "I'm not taking any patients this afternoon. I have an emergency to deal with. Reschedule them with my alternates. When Dr. Payne and Latricia Green arrive send them to my office."

They spent the entire afternoon reviewing the extensive records of the operation and the resulting deviated sleep patterns recorded in the sleep lab. Dr. Batsunappan gave her all the information he had. Latricia believed the insulative properties of myelin were not being properly reproduced. She would take the data back to Brenton Technologies for further study. After adjusting the code, Brenton Technologies would need several months of testing on live animals before trying it again on a human.

Dr. Batsunappan slumped back in his chair. "That's too long. Can't you fast track it?"

"That's with fast tracking. It's a time requirement that's closely regulated," she replied.

"I see."

"It's late. I have to get going. We'll start on it first thing tomorrow morning."

When she had gone, Dr. Payne shook his head. "Raji, I have to tell you something. Gottlieb spoke to the State Board of Physicians and there's going to be an investigation. He sent an orderly to pick up the dream portal as evidence. I have to appear at the preliminary hearing tomorrow."

"I couldn't have imagined this if I tried. He isn't blaming you, too, is he?"

"No. It's for questioning. She's your patient. Gottlieb's just got it in for you."

Dr. Batsunappan rubbed his temples with the palms of his hands. "Poor Annie. Who's going to save her?"

Dr. Payne put his hand on Batsunappan's shoulder. "I believe in what you're doing. I just don't have any choice in this."

"Tell them the truth. Don't worry about me. This is a disaster of my own making." He pulled out his desk drawer and brought out a small flash memory disk. "This is for the future. I want you to have it in case something happens to me. If it all goes bad."

Dr. Payne took the storage device and turned it over in his hand. "What do you mean, 'if it all goes bad'? What is this?"

"Dream Portal 2.0. The next leap. All the new circuitry and programming. I see where Gottlieb is going; he's going to try to bury my work. It needs to get out into the world, one way or another."

"Ah. He's just an old throwback. Don't worry. You're going to win this."

"I have a bad feeling about it. The waking world is not a logical place. That is an illusion."

Dr. Payne nodded. "It's been a crazy day. I have to get home to my family."

"You're a lucky man. Thanks, Mark."

Dr. Payne held up the disk and smiled. "I'll put it in a safe place. You'll win this."

Dr. Batsunappan wasn't hungry, but knew he'd better get some dinner to keep up his energy. If he waited much later, the restaurants would be closed. It was a problem he had as a bachelor. His work consumed all his time, both day and night, and he ate only as a necessity, sometimes missing meals. He cared for his patients, receiving their gratitude in return, and that made him happy. The pattern extended into middle age. He felt life was still rewarding, but at times a loneliness would set in and he wondered if he had made some incorrect assumptions about who he was and where he was going. He rose from his desk and turned out the lights.

As he walked by Annie's monitoring station, the technician called out: "Doctor, there's something weird about Ann Taylor's graphs. Can you take a look?"

He traced back over the readings for the last hour. The usual sawtooth and theta oscillations were there, followed by brief explosions of nightmare activity. Then long stretches of what seemed to be static filled the screen.

"I ran a diagnostic on the recorder and it's working fine," said the technician. "The electrodes are fine, too. The vital signs are good."

The doctor rubbed his chin. "The static has rhythmic spaces inside it. Like a pulse. Let's add a Z axis to graph time. " He motioned to the technician to let him sit down and typed in the new coordinate mapping. A smoothly oscillating double helix pattern appeared on the screen. "This is rich. But what does it mean?"

He walked briskly to Annie's room. Her eyes were closed and the breathing even. Her expression was serene. He had the feeling that no one was inhabiting her body; that there was a dissolution of personality. If only he still had the portal.

"I'll be back to check on her in the morning. Call me if there any more developments." His self-doubts were dissipated by the time he walked out of the clinic. For the moment, he had forgotten about the investigation.

As he feared, there were no restaurants open, so he microwaved a frozen dinner when he got home. While he sat peacefully chewing, he realized Annie's helix patterns signified a new level of consciousness; something beyond theta and deep REM. It had been days since he had communicated with her, and he needed to reach her. He remembered Lama Sri Dorbu, the Tibetan dream monk who had told of his journeys into the dream world and had mastered sheath jumping. The monk taught his followers the way to relinquish the covering of the spirit within, and travel through the other world, guided by the will. When encountering other dream beings, it was possible to enter their sheaths and exist as another. There was a danger to this, however, he had cautioned. With too many jumps, the way back to the dreamer's own covering could be lost, and the dreamer not return to the waking world.

Dr. Batsunappan was confident in his own abilities as an oneiro-naut. He had traveled in the dream world and approached other beings before. Several times he had become filled with an intense curiosity about them and contemplated jumping their sheaths. He had never taken the final leap, however. He lacked the courage and had always pulled out of the dream from fear of losing the way back.

Ann Taylor had incubated his intellectual curiosity to the point where he was willing to try Lama Sri Dorbu's ancient technique. He lay down on his bed on his right side, pulled up his knees slightly, then rested his torso on his arm and his head on his opened palm. Closing his eyes so the lids were compressed together gently, he concentrated on the points of light on the back of them. Inhaling slowly, a faint mandala formed in his field of vision. "May I awaken within this dream and grasp the fact that I am dreaming, so that all dreamlike beings may likewise awaken from the nightmare of illusory suffering and confusion." He repeated the prayer twice more, strengthening his intention to awaken within the dream each time.

The moon rose between his eyes, and he felt the energy within his body rise also to meet it. Then he was hovering, moving through the underbrush of a thick wood until he broke through at the shore of Silver Lake. On the surface of the moon a figure appeared. He willed his body to form and held out his hands, palms upward, to the moon. Its reflection played across the frozen expanse of ice and Annie skated toward him atop it, leaving snakes of shaven ice behind her as she approached.

"Welcome, Doctor!" she cried. "It's been so long. Why didn't you come sooner?"

She looked radiant in a tight-fitting skating suit covered with sequins that sparkled like stars. Something was different about her. She was stronger and more confident.

"I wanted to. But things have changed in the other world." He was unsure how to explain and how to talk about the double helix to a patient. "I wanted to check on you for one thing. Are you okay?"

Annie laughed. "I've never been better in my life. Things have changed in this world, too."

"I want you to tell me about it. But first, I must let you know that I can't be your doctor anymore. Dr. Gottlieb is going to be in charge now …" There was the sound of branches breaking. Something large and dark pushed through the trees behind him. He forced himself not to look. Dr. Batsunappan realized that he was the source of the disturbance.

Annie saw it, too, and skated to the edge of the ice thrusting her hands out toward him. "You better get on the ice, Doctor."

"I can't skate, Annie."

"You can do whatever you want. You taught me about The Maker. Remember?"

He willed skates on his feet and glided onto the ice. The thing resorbed into the woods. "Will you teach me to skate?"

She took his hands and began skating backward, pulling him along. "But you already know how." She released him like ammunition from a sling and he shot forward. He skated on his own beside her.

A happy smile spread across the older man's face which he quickly erased in embarrassment. "I want you to know that programmers are working on the device that was implanted in you. But it may be a long time until they can apply the fix. It's something about the regulations…"

They stopped together in a shower of ice. "Don't try to save me. I'm not going back. There are more worlds in this place than you can conceive of. Dreams of dreams, world after world. Let me show them to you."

The doctor saw the joy in her face and didn't know what to say. He shook his head slowly. "There are things I must do. I have to go back."

"Are you too old to hope? Those *things* are an illusion."

He frowned sternly. "I'm fifteen years your senior and I am telling you that you will return to the real world. I will tell you what an illusion is and what it is not. We are going to save you."

"No, Doctor. Who will save you from yourself? You can return to your world of brick and mortar if you want to, but not me"

She skated toward the moon and disappeared into its light. The dreamscape shimmered and dissipated. Dr. Batsunappan heard his phone ringing and picked it up on the last ring. It was 3 a.m.

"We lost the readout completely, but her vitals are fine," said the technician. "We switched over to another station. Same thing."

"I'm on my way," said the doctor.

It was still dark when he arrived at the clinic. Dr. Batsunappan grunted his greeting to the technician and hurried down the hall to Annie's room. Her body was glowing with health as he looked down upon her, but once more it didn't seem inhabited. He returned to the monitoring station and scrutinized the last hour of readouts. The double helix corresponded to the brief period when he had entered her dream on the lake. The rest was a straight solid line which indicated no mental activity of any kind.

"Is she okay?" asked the technician. "What's going on?"

"I don't know. It could be an interaction with the liquid metal implant. I'm not sure. Keep a close eye out for any more changes."

He was the first one in the cafeteria and had to wait for the coffee to finish brewing. After breakfast he went to his office and checked his patients' records to make sure all the i's were dotted and the t's crossed. Putting off Mr. Harrison's for last, he went through the cancer patient's records thoroughly to reassure himself that the consent form had been filled out properly. He realized with a sinking heart, that the neuro-translator had not been identified as an experimental medical device and every byte of information on the use of it had left a time-stamped electronic trail back to him.

The medical board was probably pouring over Harrison's records at this moment. And Ann Taylor's as Mark Payne was answering their questions.

Dr. Batsunappan opened his research paper on the dream portal and scrolled to where he had left off. A few more weeks of work remained until it would be ready to submit. There was no way he could beat the old white hair to the punch and prove him to be the doddering reactionary that he was. At least Mark was on his side and had the plans for the new dream portal.

Dr. Batsunappan began a new chapter: The Fallacy of Brain Mapping. Late in the afternoon the mail chime sounded. A registered email had arrived from the State of Maryland Medical Board of Examiners. He was to appear before them immediately to formally surrender his license to practice in the State of Maryland. In the interim he was disbarred from practicing medicine and was to turn over all patients and records to Dr. John Gottlieb.

He clasped his hands together and took several deep breaths. Anger would serve no purpose. Gottlieb needed to be told to step aside for progress and innovation. He was the one to tell him. The old throwback needed to know that he should not harbor grudges against those who had a future because he had no vision himself. Dr. Batsunappan called the senior physician's office to tell him these things, but there was no answer. The white-hair had already gone home.

Dr. Batsunappan returned to his writing and continued to work late into the night. When the chapter was finished, he saved it to a memory disk and shut off the computer. He clasped the disk tightly and walked to the window. Outside was the world of brick and mortar. The old Queen Ann row houses of Baltimore lined the streets several stories below, their lights winking in the darkness. He realized his demise would lead to the appointment of a new director for Clear Light Sleep Technologies, and that it, in all probability, would not survive.

He turned off the office lights and walked to the monitoring station for Annie. Her readout had not changed. Still a straight line. "No change, doctor," said the technician. "Have you figured it out?"

He smiled wryly. "Perhaps. Check me into Room 11. I'm too tired to drive home. I need to make up for lost sleep."

Dr. Batsunappan shut the door to the room next to Annie's and set the disk containing his nearly finished paper on the night table where he hoped it would be noticed. He lay on the empty bed. Pulling his knees up, he rested his head on his opened palm, inhaling and exhaling slowly. He was very tired and immediately the mandala formed in his field of vision. "May I awaken within this dream and grasp the fact that I am dreaming, so that all dreamlike beings may likewise awaken from the nightmare of illusory suffering and confusion."

Before he had a chance to chant a second time, the moon rose. He appeared on the shore of the frozen lake and held up his palms. "Annie." Looking across the lake, the stillness of winter warmed his heart. He glided in silence across the silent ice, gaining speed. "Annie."

He looked up from the blue moonbeams painted into the ice and was amazed by the fullness of the stars, sparkling in infinity. When he looked down, she was beside him.

"Doctor, you've come. I have so much to show you."

"I'm not a doctor anymore. Call me Raji."

Awaken - Episode 4:
Maryland House

A trailer marked with faded letters on the sides reading AASHTO sat on the parking lot of the southbound side of the Maryland House rest stop. Inside was the National Security Committee: ten stern women and men watching a man working at a control console on the wall. "We have a new tool in our arsenal, a magic crystal," Dr. Payne said, making adjustments as he paused between each word. He turned to face his audience to make sure they were still listening.

"We've got a lot on the plate so let's get on with it," demanded a medal-bedecked general.

Standing next to the general was Director Drendlen, a sallow-complexioned man with puffy lips and thick spectacles. "The committee has been briefed on the Maryland House Project already, doctor. What we need is a successful demonstration, that's all. If it works, we'll buy it. Very simple. Everyone here has clearance, so go ahead, speak freely."

Dr. Payne took a deep breath and slowly exhaled. He had waited years for this moment. Years of research and planning had been invested. The time had come to convince them it would work. "I'll be to the point. Our surveillance systems are too expensive with too few results. The Kennen crystal satellites now in use are obsolete. With Director Drendlen's permission, I've arranged a demonstration of a radically new system that will totally change our intelligence gathering. Our magic crystal is no longer a satellite orbiting overhead, trying to second guess what's going on down on the ground. Now it's in the middle of the action, implanted inside the subject's head, looking, hearing, feeling everything he or she interacts with."

"Are you talking about some kind of bug?" asked a thin man in a dark suit.

"Yes, in a sense. It communicates neurological signals in both directions, however." There was silence. Dr. Payne coughed and continued. "But it goes far beyond conventional bugs. It manipulates the thoughts and actions of an individual undetected. The best thing is to show you the system in action."

A map of the Washington – Baltimore corridor popped up on the screen showing a vehicle approaching the rest stop from the northbound lane of Route 95.

"Director Drendlen has identified a known subversive named George Anders to work with for our pilot study. He's a keynote speaker at the demonstration in Philadelphia. Anders is the president of the Worldwide Worker's Union Mid-Atlantic Division. We've ID'd his car nearby on the GPS grid and surveillance records show that he often stops here when traveling Route 95. We'll implant the device when he gets here, monitor the subject's activity, and alter his actions and decisions to produce whatever consequences are deemed appropriate by Director Drendlen."

The committee members pulled up seats in a semi-circle in front of the console as the lights dimmed. Dr. Payne stepped aside and pointed to the control console. "Ladies and gentlemen, I give you the Maryland House Project."

George and his wife, Alice, had slumped back in their seats, resigned to the monotony of autopilot during the long trip from Richmond, Virginia. He tugged at the TV cover which slid inside the dashboard, displaying the 2044 presidential debate in progress.

"I'm glad we agree on politics," said Alice. "I would divorce you if you became one of them."

George opened a bag of malted milk balls and began crunching them between the fillings of his teeth. "Yeah. If they win this one we're back to the robber barons of the 1800's."

"That's why this march is so important. I just hope it doesn't snow," Alice replied.

"It's too cold to snow. When it's below 20 degrees you never get a real snow, maybe just a flurry or two."

She held out her hand for a malt ball. "Where did you hear that?"

"I just noticed it. It's common sense."

"Well, I don't like the cold, whether it snows or not. If it does, it'll at least show how dedicated everyone is – to walk for miles in it and all. I hope they stick around for your speech."

George opened the refrigerator and pulled out a soda, offering it to Alice. She accepted and he pulled one out for himself. When the last malt ball slid down his throat and the can was empty, he began fumbling with the GPS, trying to get their location.

"What's the matter?" she asked.

"My bladder is out of control. We got to take a pit stop."

Alice glanced out the window. "Maryland House is coming up."

"Punch it in, will you?"

She touched the lighted Maryland House button displayed on the screen under Rest Stops. A few minutes later the autopilot began braking and the whine of the car's flywheel increased in pitch as it recaptured the forward momentum of the vehicle.

They were diverted into the parking lot along with several dozen other cars. George disconnected and found a lucky spot about 400 meters from the northbound ramp. He and Alice melded into the dense swell of travelers heading for the doors. As they entered, they passed by an antique penny flattening machine.

"Who would want to flatten a penny? They're worth a small fortune. Meet you back here," said George.

She veered toward the ladies' room and George made his way to the men's. He scanned the wall, frantically looking for an opening, and picked a urinal with only two in line. When his turn came, he stepped forward and let the dam break. A camera mounted in the ceiling zoomed in on the back of his head, which appeared on a display in the console of the trailer.

"This is the implant," said Dr. Payne, pointing to three fine hairs falling from the scalp onto George's collar.

"We can't see anything, Doctor," said Drendlen. "Can you point it out?"

Dr. Payne zoomed in closer. An insect less than the size of a gnat began depositing a round dot smaller than a pore on George's scalp. The dot burrowed into the flesh without a trace. "We borrowed a UAS – a nano drone – from you guys for the delivery. That part of the technology is already proven. But the little dot that you all saw for a moment is why you are here today. It's the latest in piezo-electric liquid crystallography. It liquefies, finds its way through the scalp and bone, and enters the brain. We activate the interface, and everything going on inside the subject's head is transmitted back to us." Dr. Payne pushed a button on the panel. "Anders is our eyes and ears."

George was busy with the business at hand. For a split second, he felt something like a mosquito bite on the back of his head. He forgot about it at once, it passed so quickly. The perspective shifted from the ceiling to a point two feet from the wall and the sound of flushing was heard.

"Excuse me," said George, while pulling up his fly and backing away from the urinal, side stepping the man behind him.

"So, what's supposed to happen?" asked the general. "I only see some guy taking a leak."

"That's the beauty of it, General," said Dr. Payne. "It's so fast it's undetectable and the implant is so small, there's no pain or mark of any kind. And we all shed a little sometimes."

The bald general did not respond to the humor, but Dr. Payne plowed on, trying to win his audience. "It has happened. You aren't looking through the camera anymore, you're inside the subject's head, experiencing what he experiences. His brain waves are being sent to us right now, here in this room, and translated by our system into human terms of perception like sight, sound and feelings."

The room remained silent. Dr. Payne was fearful he was losing them. "That's only a small part of what it can do." With cool correctness, he extended a metal pointer and tapped on an area of the console filled with graphs. "These depict emotional and psychological states. This is the strength of input and output signals from the subject's brain to our control center here. This one indicates serotonin levels, pain, pleasure, motivation, and last, but not least, sexual stimulation."

"What's the range of this thing?" asked the thin man.

"As long as our satellites are operational, unlimited."

"You mentioned 'manipulate' thoughts and actions – how does that work?"

"Good question," said Dr. Payne. "Back in the 1980's a British researcher, named Greene, identified the parts of the human nervous system that send and receive nerve impulses. Greene was ahead of his time. He hooked up the outputs of his own nerves to those of paraplegics and was able to control their limbs. In another experiment, he connected electrodes in a patient's brain to a computer and trained him to move the cursor across the screen. It is only recently that we have developed the technical components to put his findings to practical use. We built on Greene's discoveries and incorporated them into our system using the latest piezoelectric technology and something new called a neuro-translator. We monitor the subject's brain patterns, digitize them, rearrange them and play back our modified version to induce any thought, speech or action that we choose. Since it's only their own modified brain pattern, they can't detect the change. They're under our control and never know it."

Helen Buffini, legal counsel to the National Security Committee, rose indignantly from her seat. "Dr. Payne, really. Mind control?"

"Total mind control, well, no. But manipulation, yes. It also can influence sex drive, mood, outlook, sleep – personality."

"We could shoot this thing into the heads of the enemy from the air and march 'em right back the hell home," said the general.

"There are enormous possibilities, General," said Director Drendlen. "This is just the beginning. We've only begun to study ways of applying it. That's why we set up the project. Mr. Anders will help us learn what the implant can do and where we can take it."

"Director Drendlen," said the counselor.

The director continued, ignoring her. "While Mr. Anders is on his way to the demonstration..."

"Director Drendlen," she repeated angrily.

"Yes, Ms. Buffini. What?"

"This is barbaric and illegal. It's also a violation of free speech."

"Thank you for your opinion, but no, it's top secret medical research."

"I have to inform you as legal counselor you are on thin ice. If this gets out there could be a scandal."

Director Drendlen scowled. "There is no chance of that happening. It's classified and will never leave this room. This is medical research, funded as such with blessings from the highest places."

They continued to watch the display. George and Alice climbed back into their car and drove to the exit ramp.

"You want to go over your speech again? I'll read along," said Alice.

"You always get sick reading in the car."

She pulled up the document on her cell phone. "Not always. Go ahead."

George's face grew serious. He paused, waiting for the feeling of conviction to come, then looked up as he remembered the words he had prepared:

"I'm honored to be here today. Honored that you, my fellow workers, have asked me to speak on your behalf on this cold day, about something we all share; the right to a livelihood, to a decent standard of living; to fair labor laws that ensure uniform standards of decency for all people throughout the world.

"We are the Worldwide Workers Union. Everywhere on this globe, in every continent, we have fought for the rights of all workers to be safe and healthy, and to receive decent wages, training and education to maintain the highest professional standards. We stand for the end of child labor and the abolishment of prison labor.

"More importantly, we stand united and determined that this administration will not succeed in its attempts to abolish labor unions and take us back to the past which we had fought so hard to escape from. We must not rest until the unregulated toil of children and the under trodden of every nation, has been eliminated from the face of the earth. It is our duty to elevate the social conscience of government leadership to the betterment of all members of society...."

"You getting this, Dr. Payne?" asked Director Drendlen.

"It's going into memory right now," the doctor replied.

Director Drendlen faced the semi-circle. "We're all on the same page here. This is not the kind of message we want broadcast around the globe. This subversion must be stopped in its tracks and now we have the tool to do it. The Maryland House Project must succeed, it's vital to our national interest. I know how busy you all are and don't want to detain you any longer. We'll reconvene tomorrow at the same time."

"I think Ms. Buffini doesn't like the Maryland House Project," Dr. Payne commented sadly after she had left.

"She'll come around. She has to play ball with the administration or she's out of a job. Do we have the whole speech yet?" Drendlen asked.

"He's finished. We can start the modification."

"Good. Play it back. Then start feeding him some behavioral reinforcements that will make him ... more like one of us."

"It's too soon for that," said Dr. Payne. "It'll take time to change his outlook and behavior, that's a gradual thing. But we can have him reciting our speech whenever we choose."

The director listened intently as George's speech played back, writing on a notepad the whole time.

"He's in Philadelphia now," said Dr. Payne. "It's a half hour until speech time."

"Just finishing up. Pipe this into his brain." He handed the altered version to Dr. Payne.

A few minutes later George and Alice were being directed into a tight parking spot on Front Street by someone who had stepped out of a bagel shop.

"Look who it is, Larry Phillips himself," sneered Drendlen. "Damned subversive. You saving all this?"

"We're getting everything."

"We were turned down for a permit again," said Larry as he helped pull George's bulk out of the car. "But we didn't let that stop us. At least 450,000 marchers. The press is covering it all."

"How close are they?" asked George.

"They passed the Liberty Bell ten minutes ago. They'll reach Penn's Landing in a few minutes."

"We better get to the stage then," said George.

They walked along Front Street toward Penn's Landing. As they mounted the aluminum scaffolding of the stage the marchers came into view. The police had erected fences along the sidewalks and intersections, packing the demonstrators more densely in the street. The crowd stretched back from the landing as far as the eye could see. Giant display screens hung from poles at the intersections. The speakers were standing in a group near the center of the stage. On the stage was a podium with a dozen mounted microphones. Media cameras swept in all directions to capture the event as it unfolded.

Larry Phillips and George Anders stood near the podium as the marchers filed up the landing and came to a halt. The air swelled with the chant "all the world is one."

Larry walked to the podium as snow began to fall through the frigid air. He raised his hands and spoke into the mics. "My friends. Thank you for coming to show your support for our cause. You endured a long march through the wind and cold today. Each one of you began your journey here with a single step. From every state in this country, and from every country in the world, you got here one step at a time. That is how we will win back our representation, one heart and one mind at a time. We shall not stop until we reach our destination: fairness and equality for all! Thank you for your perseverance and for your commitment and determination. You will not be disappointed. Today you'll hear from our brothers and sisters from all over the world: Sri Kemchandanni of the WWWU of India, Mike Nakishemma of Japan, Henry Muller of Germany, and others. Now, here to begin this event, is our president of the Mid-Atlantic Region, USA, George Anders!"

George lumbered to the podium. He looked down the long blocks of humanity, standing silently in the falling snow. At the foot of the stage Alice's upturned face looked into his. They exchanged smiles through the snowflakes.

George turned to the waiting camera and felt the conviction coming. He opened his mouth to speak....

"Transmit," said Drendlen.

Dr. Payne nodded. "Connected and transmitting."

"I am honored to be here today," said George. "Honored that you, my fellow workers, have asked me to speak on your behalf this cold day, about something we all share; the right to a livelihood; to a decent standard of living; to fair labor laws that ensure uniform standards of decency for all people throughout the world.

"But I have been thinking long and deeply on the Worldwide Workers Union and its cause. After much consideration, I've reevaluated my position and have come to believe we are on the wrong course to achieve the things we want."

Larry looked at George with raised eyebrows. George had always been a man of words, not of action. He wore his usual cherubic look that made him believable and convincing. "I hope the punch line is good," said Larry into George's ear.

George continued, unruffled. "We all carry within us the seeds of creativity. We have the right to exercise it, the right to innovate, the right to build and to succeed. The spark is within each of us, we are all Titans, every one of us. Do we want to regulate the spark? Are we all to be forced to be the same by law? What are we afraid of? I'll tell you what we're afraid of...."

"Traitor," someone yelled. A shoe struck George on the chest. He picked it up and turned it over, bewilderment spreading across his face. "We're afraid of hoping for more," he continued, dropping the shoe and looking out at the crowd again. "We need to trust in the leadership that has the vision and courage to deliver to us what we all need deep down...."

"Where you going with this? That's fucking crap man!" shouted a protestor in the crowd.

"How much they payin' you?" yelled another.

"Thank you, George, we've heard enough," said Larry sarcastically. He grabbed George by the shoulder and forced him away from the podium.

"I'm not finished," said George struggling back to the mics, but Larry and an aide shoved him away.

"Oh no, you're finished," Larry snarled. "Get him out of here."

The aide grabbed George's arm and walked him down the stairs.

Larry spoke into the mics as Sri Kemchandanni stepped to the podium. "We're going to hear from a man who has been a bridge over troubled waters, our colleague and ally from India, Sri Kemchandanni."

As Kemchandanni addressed the crowd, Larry shot down the steps. "After all the years I've known you, you've decided to turn traitor now, at this moment? You never said a word to anybody about your epiphany. Why?"

George's eyes opened wide. "What the hell are you talking about?"

"That wasn't the speech you were going to give," said Alice. "George, don't you know what you just said?" She repeated his last line.

"I said that?" asked George.

Part of the crowd broke off and began surrounding George and Alice.

"Traitor. Somebody paid you off. You're working for them now. Who's payin' you, traitor?"

"Nobody," said George, unable to accept the unfolding nightmare.

One of the marchers pushed George backward into the stage and raised his fist. Alice screamed, then George grabbed her hand and started running away as the others restrained the protester from further violence. The police came barreling through, pushing people aside with their storm shields. Alice and George ran down the street and disappeared into the snow while the police battled a mounting insurrection of angry marchers.

In a small Georgetown bistro, Director Drendlen and Dr. Payne sat at a table near a TV in the corner of the room. They ordered dinner as the seven o'clock news came on.

"This ought to be good," said the director.

"The food or the news?"

"Both."

Standing in front of a burning police car, the commentator began her report: "A demonstration by the Worldwide Workers Union has ended in mayhem as hundreds of demonstrators wrestle with police. Trash cans have been emptied to create a bonfire in the middle of the street, and this police car in back of me set on fire. Tear gas was used to subdue the unruly agitators and dozens of arrests have been made. The violence began shortly after the keynote speaker, Mr. George Anders, denounced the direction the WWWU has been taking and advocated a mainstream outlook. One of the union members had to be pulled away from manhandling Mr. Anders, who fled with a woman, presumably his wife. His whereabouts is still unknown. Sandy King reporting live from Penn's Landing, Philadelphia."

Dr. Payne smiled. "The doctor knows best."

"So how can you change his behavior and outlook?"

"It's like training a dog," said Dr. Payne. "Reward him for good behavior. Only instead of a pat on the head, we feed him pleasure directly into his brain. We learn his pleasure frequencies then redirect them back. It can be better than an orgasm or heroin rush. We regulate the level of pleasure depending on the kind of reinforcement we need. He'll want to act in the way that brings the greatest pleasure."

The food arrived and the director became cordial. "So, tell me, how far can we take this thing? I mean, it could be used in a lot of ways, right?"

Dr. Payne pulled a mussle from its shell and inspected it on his fork. "It has great potential in medicine and psychotherapy. I'm working on a new version that doesn't need a console. There's almost no limit."

"What is it that you want out of all of this?"

Dr. Payne thought for a second. "Just recognition."

"You want to go down in medical history, you mean?"

"That's right. Everything else will follow. Funding. My own company."

"Interesting," said Director Drendlen, nodding his head. The director tapped his fingers on the table and leaned closer. "Now me, I just want to serve my country. And protect it. The Maryland House Project is bigger than you and me and it's a double-edged sword. It's like when we learned to split the atom; good can come of it, but in the wrong hands great harm can be done." He put his hand on the doctor's shoulder. "We have to make sure it stays in the right hands. It's in the national interest. Not a word gets out. It stays within the project committee. I want your solemn word on that."

The doctor frowned and swallowed another mussle.

"Cheer up, we'll see you get the recognition you deserve."

Dr. Payne nodded reluctantly.

George and Alice drove home exhausted. The dash TV filled them in on the upheaval in Philadelphia. Larry Phillips had vanished. George had become an instant celebrity and the media pundits speculated endlessly on his sudden awakening to mainstream ideology.

"Did I really say that?" A pleasant feeling of warmth came over him.

"You did, but did you mean it?" asked Alice.

"Funny, I don't know," he said, furrowing his brow.

"That wasn't in your speech. You just couldn't change like that – could you?"

The warm feeling got stronger.

"Your eyes are big," said Alice.

George looked in the rear-view mirror. His eyes were dilated and shiny. "So what?"

They lapsed into a silence that was unbroken all the way home. Still incommunicado, they parked and took the elevator to their condominium on the eighteenth floor and marched woodenly to bed.

George got up at seven the next morning according to habit, then headed for the union office. The place had a different feel about it. The receptionist wished him a cold good morning as he walked past to the elevator. When he got to his office, the door was locked.

"I wasn't sure you would show up here again after your speech," said Pete Johnson, union vice president, opening the door. Two security guards stood behind him.

"Pete, didn't you ever think it might be time to bury the hatchet and begin closing the gap. The world can't be divided forever.

We're the leaders, we got to do something to bring the two sides together." As he spoke, a subtle warmth flowed through his veins.

Johnson looked out the window. A news van was pulling up to the front lobby door. He stepped aside and pointed to George. "Get him out of here; take him out the back. Don't let him talk to any reporters."

The guards hooked arms with George and dragged him down the hall on his heels to the back stairs. "Let's not end it this way, Pete," pleaded George. "Not after all these years. Come on, just talk to me for a minute." His eyes were the size of saucers.

Johnson shook his head. "We used to share the same dream. I used to respect you. We have nothing to talk about anymore. Don't come back."

Without taking his eyes off the control console, Director Drendlen picked up a cup of coffee and took a swig. "You've got mine. I don't take sugar," he said.

Dr. Payne finished adjusting the volume, then swapped cups. "He's not convincing in this state; his eyes are too dilated. It needs to take place more slowly, over a longer period. We've tried to do too much, too fast."

"That's the end of our mole," said Director Drendlen.

"We can still use him as a figurehead. He's got the media going and they all want to interview him."

The director rubbed his nose and adjusted his glasses. "No, he's just going to draw suspicion. People will think he's crazy or maybe even brainwashed."

"Should we bring him in, hide him for a while?"

Drendlen threw his cup in the trash. "Terminate him."

Dr. Payne stared incredulously. "You can't."

"Not me. He can do himself in. Just a little nudge in the right direction is all that's needed. It would look natural and help discredit their leadership. He would only seem more imbalanced. A sudden switch of ideology, suddenly feeling like a betrayer and unable to live with himself he might even...."

"He was neutralized as a political leader yesterday at the demonstration. There's no need for that. I'd call that a success."

Director Drendlen cocked his head and smiled. "You will terminate George Anders tonight. That's if you want backing for the Maryland House Project so you can get the recognition you deserve."

Dr. Payne stared back blankly. "I'll think of something. It'll look natural."

"I know I can count on you."

At the Anders' home there was a note on the table when George returned: Have to get away for a few days to think things out. – Alice.

George slumped into a chair and lowered his head on his arms, sobbing. The warm feeling had left hours ago, replaced by a paralyzing, numbing cold. *Why?* he wondered. *What have I done? I've lost everything.* It crushed his senses, putting out everything. The silence filled the space around him, leaving no room to breathe. He had to get out, once and for all.

When he got up from the table it was 3:00 am. George walked out the balcony door. The night was clear and the stars looked down in cold silence. He grabbed a column and stepped up on the rail, peering over the side. The ground below was empty and he let go. For an instant he was in Philadelphia, watching the march.

"No, George!" cried Alice.

A hand clamped his collar and pulled him backward onto the balcony. Something metal banged down on his head.

"We figured it out buddy, keep the helmet on," said Larry Phillips.

"What the hell is this?" shouted George, struggling to tear off the helmet while Larry pressed it down harder.

"Take a couple of deep breaths and calm down. You have to keep it on," said Alice. "Tell him Larry."

"When Alice showed me your written speech, the one you intended to give, we knew someone was fucking with your mind."

"Nobody was fucking with my mind," said George.

"You know, like in the movie, The Lawnmower Man, slicing off brain cells with a lawnmower inside someone's head. We figured something happened to you on your way to Penn's Landing. Then I got a call from a woman in Washington, Helen Buffini, who said you were part of a medical experiment. There's a lab in a trailer at Maryland House travel center where they put some kind of implant in your head. They control your mind with it."

"They used you," said Alice. "They changed your speech. When you weren't any more use to them, they brought you out here to...."

"Snuff it." George hugged Alice. "Thank you. I feel like I'm coming up from the bottom of the ocean. I'm me again. You too, Larry. Thank you."

"Just keep the helmet on, it's steel and blocks the signal. Let's get back inside and think about what we're going to do," said Larry.

They sat at the kitchen table. Except for the crunching of malted milk balls between George's teeth, it was dead quiet. George swallowed and broke the silence.

"Now that I can think for myself again, I'm getting some ideas. Let's beat them at their own game. They used the media against us, now we can use it against them."

"Who is them?" asked Alice.

"I don't know," said George.

Larry tapped on George's helmet. "Don't forget our friend on the inside. I'll ask Helen Bufinni."

"Larry, can you arrange a meeting between us, Helen Bufinni, and the media? Maybe a big name like Sandy King?" asked George.

Larry nodded. "Let's do it in their own lair, right there at Maryland House. It would be headline stuff. I'll arrange it."

George proffered malt balls to Alice and Larry. Each crunched a mouthful in agreement.

Larry Phillips arranged the meeting for that afternoon. The news crew, Helen Bufinni, George, Alice and Larry converged at the penny flattener by the doors of the rest stop.

"Mr. Anders, I'm glad you agreed to meet with us first. It's a strange story, but we'll check it out," said Sandy King. She nodded to the cameraman to start recording. "Let me explain to our viewers that Mr. Anders, whom many of you may remember from the worldwide worker's demonstration in Philadelphia two days ago, has claimed that he is the victim of a mind control experiment conducted upon him from a trailer in the parking lot here at the Maryland House travel center near Exit 80 in Aberdeen. We're standing at the entrance now."

The camera swung to George. "I keep asking myself if this is really happening," said George, looking into the camera. "I have trouble believing it myself. I'm just trying to cope and want to get to the bottom of it like everyone else. The speech was not my speech. The public must understand that. I want to know how they did this to me and get them out of my head, that's all. I'm a victim of mind control by our government."

The camera shifted back to the reporter. "Ms. Helen Buffini is a legal advisor to the National Security Council and has taken on the role of whistle blower. She agreed to talk with us about these allegations." She held the mic toward the counselor.

"It's true," Helen Buffini confirmed. "There are large issues at stake here which need to be brought to the public's attention. This experiment is an invasion of Mr. Ander's personal privacy and a violation of freedom of speech conducted without his consent."

"Isn't it true that this is classified as top secret? Aren't you breaking the law by breaking the code of silence regarding classified government projects?" asked the reporter as they made their way through the parking lot.

"I'm willing to do the right thing, no matter what the cost," the counselor replied. She led the group to the trailer door and punched in the code for the lock. Dr. Payne and nine surprised committee members turned to face them. "Hello, Director," she said.

Director Drendlen instructed Dr. Payne to turn off the display screens and dashed across the room waving his hands in the air. "Ms. Bufinni, what are you doing bringing these people in here? You know this is a classified project." He forced a smile.

George held out a box of malt balls. "Care for one, Director Drendlen?"

Drendlen's smile faded. "Nice hat fella."

"Vintage Hell's Angels, World War Two surplus. What have you done to me? Get out of my head!"

Sandy King stuck the mic in Drendlen's face. "Director Drendlen, Mr. Anders claims he is the victim of a medical experiment to control his thoughts and speech. Is this true? Would you care to comment on his accusation?"

"I'm not commenting on anything. You've entered a classified area without clearance. Leave here at once." A quadcopter landed outside and five MPs jumped out onto the asphalt.

Drendlen grabbed the camera from the cameraman's hand as the intruders were shoved out of the trailer into the parking lot.

As the counselor and her entourage returned to their cars, the cameraman held up a memory module containing the video session. "We better get out of here before he notices the camera's empty."

"Are we going to be on the news tonight?" asked Larry.

"Yes, but we can't use the shots inside the trailer," said Sandy King. "It's a federal offense without a court order."

"It's proof. We've got to show it," said George.

Helen shook her head. "Sandy would incriminate herself. That's a top-secret area."

"I'll leak it somehow," said the reporter. "Helen, I want to do an exclusive interview with you tonight. Would you be willing?"

"Of course."

"Come on, let's get back to the station. You can ride with me." She thought she felt something bite her on the top of her head as she got in the van, but decided to ignore it. Helen Buffini climbed in after her and slid the door closed. She heard a tiny buzz, and in that instant, realized it was too late.

Inside the trailer, Director Drendlen placed his hand on Dr. Payne's shoulder. "Thank you, doctor. I knew I could count on you."

Rust

L iz, the rentable office worker, smiled from her fifty foot high billboard at the corrugated exterior of Wilson Industrial Supply down below. LIZ IS ALL ABOUT YOU, YOU, YOU glared in mind blast lettering through the race of passing windshields into the heads of motorists traveling the overpass. The beams and supports they were suspended on came from the labor of steel workers in shops across the country like the one hidden beneath them. Jimmy, a wiry veteran with oversized forearms, turned away from the parts room window to avoid her eyes and flipped the calendar hanging above his desk from Miss June to Miss July. "Wow, I'll bet she's high maintenance."

Miss American Steel of the Month stood in front of a pool, showing off a perfect tan in a scant bikini, her delicate hand caressing a steel pillar erected in concrete. Pop Korn stared. "Bet she's got a sugar daddy."

"Maybe even a CEO with a golden parachute."

The furrows of the old man's forehead deepened. "Golden parachute?"

"That's what happens when they downsize. The CEOs get twenty million – like at Fairless Hills Steel. My dad worked there. They sold it to some investor and moved the equipment to China.

He got sent over there and trained the Chinese to run it. Then they laid him off. The CEO got twenty million so he wouldn't get distracted from making the hard decisions. Closing the factory being one of them."

"That so." Korn opened the doors to a beat-up parts cabinet streaked with paint runs and took out a torch tip. He signed the checkout sheet on Jimmy's desk, but before he could leave, a lanky form emerged through the door. The head wore a knowing grin accentuated by a grizzle that was almost a goatee. The grizzle made him seem older than he was. Chad bent his stick thin torso and spat on the floor. "Got somethin' for ya Korn. Charlie ain't comin' back. So, you're drivin' truck."

"I hope he's gone for good. He's one crazy muthafugga'. He took part da yard lift and de bucket an neva put 'em back. Nuthin' works round here now cause a dat asshole."

"'Till we hire somebody new," said Chad, "you're gonna run steel up to Maryland. There's a job box goin' up too. I'll get directions for you." He tilted his head and spat again. "Jimmy, you an' Korn go 'round back an' hook up the trailer'."

"Right," Jimmy said.

In the back yard were parked two stake body trucks and a twenty-five foot trailer. A bucket truck and giant yard lift rested nearby, their rusting hulks partially disassembled.

"Charlie was a crazy muthafugga an' ova-loaded dem trucks – bent da fuggin' frame on dis stakebody. See da bed ain't even wif da cab – see dat?" Korn pointed to the space between the cab and the bed where the truck visibly sagged in the middle. "I tol' 'em, 'You gonna bend da frame – won't hold more'n six beam guides.' He said, 'It'll be fine, it'll be fine.' Well look, fuggin' frame's bent. He put twelve dem muthafuggers on – dat's twelve thousand pounds. Asshole!"

"Yeah. He killed it, alright. Guess that's why he disappeared instead of quitting. That would have been the decent thing to do." Jimmy hoisted his small frame into the only drivable stake body and started the engine.

"Come on back, cut it," said Pop Korn, twisting an invisible wheel to the right. "Ho." He turned the hitch crank, raising the coupling an inch, then motioned to come back again.

The coupler slid under the eye and Pop Korn locked the clamp, then plugged in the tail-light connector. Jimmy put on the turn signal and hollered out the window: "How's the turn signals. They blinkin'?"

"No."

"What about the brake light?"

Korn shook his head. "No."

Jimmy drove the truck to the front yard. The sun beat down on piled beams that returned the rays in amplified waves of heat. His forehead was beaded in sweat as he walked through the front bay into the buzz of wheel cutters combined with the deep pounding of a twenty-ton press and the din of milling machines. A smoky haze hung in the air despite the fact the doors were wide open on each end of the hangar-like building. Each day of the last thirty years the haze deposited a new layer of sticky funk on everything inside.

Jimmy squinted into the dimness at Chad who pointed to a framework of welded girders. "Lucky and Queball are finishin' the paint, so you and Korn get this here frame on the stake body and dog it down. Then you come back an' get the long ones when the paint's dry an' put 'em on the trailer'."

"The trailer lights are out and the back tires are dry-rotted, Chad. Think we can get 'em fixed?"

Chad's goatee stood up on his chin. "From lookin' 'round here, would you say they want to spend money on anything?"

Jimmy shook his head and jumped in the seat of an electric lift and headed for the girders. Out in the yard, he raised the forks to their full extension to clear the stake body's sides and position it over the middle of the bed. The lift contacted the side, then he lowered the load.

Queball drove a lift with a stack of steel sheets through the doors and pulled next to Jimmy. "You can take that off so I can put these underneath."

"What the hell you been smokin' Queball? They're not on the job order."

Queball's bald head shone in the heat. "They are now, white boy."

"Chad just added them," said Lucky, trailing in behind Queball. "And the beams are dry. You can load them, too."

Jimmy grunted, then raised the framework and pulled the lift away. After the sheets were placed on the bed and the framework reloaded, Pop Korn threw a set of lanyards over them and Lucky set the hooks in anchor holes on the other side. Pop Korn worked the ratchets until the straps were dogged so tight they pinged when you plucked them. He leaned toward Jimmy. "Queball's got a fuggin' damn mouth on 'im."

Jimmy nodded. "I noticed that."

After the trailer was full to capacity with twenty-foot beams, Jimmy handed Korn a set of directions. "Watch out for traffic in Washington."

Pop Korn stepped up into the cab and started the engine. "I ain't settin' no speed records."

The heat was hard to ignore. After ordering supplies over the phone, Jimmy got up from his desk and stood in front of the fan. It was blowing hot air and did little to cool him off. It reminded him of the hot winds which preceded the sand storms when he was stationed in Iraq.

"Hotter 'n hell," said Lucky, coming in to get a faceplate for his welding mask.

"Not as hot as Iraq. The wind was like a hair dryer blowin' on you. Then we'd get these sand storms. They were more like grit storms. It got into everything."

"Remind me not to go there."

Jimmy leaned into the blowing air and closed his eyes. "When I got out of the service I got hired by a contractor. $80,000 a year."

"No shit. Do-in' what?"

"Packing ammo. Loading missiles."

Lucky wiped the sweat hanging from his nose with his sleeve. "You must be rich."

"Never saved a cent. My wife divorced me while I was over there. She and her boyfriend put it up their noses."

"That's a bite, man."

The drone of the fan had a mesmerizing effect on Jimmy that released unpleasant memories against his will. He and his buddies emerged back in the same re-run loading aircraft missiles. A fifteen-foot missile came loose from a pallet and started rolling across the runway as he approached with a fork lift. There was no time to reverse or run. A metallic ringing rose in pitch until it collided with the sharp points of the forks. The forks pierced through both sides, missing the detonator by a quarter inch. They laughed hysterically when they realized they were still alive.

He still would go back if there was someone who cared about his boys and him. But Linda changed while he was in the Middle East. She somehow fell in with a bunch of dopers.

He remembered when he was on leave and he had walked out on his front porch during the winter. There was a stalagmite of frozen yellow piss standing up on the doormat. An old Firebird with a boom box thudding a war chant laid wheels down the street. He heard Linda and her boyfriend laughing as they pulled away.

Jimmy leaned into the simoom blast of the fan. "He wants a fight, but if I do, she'll stick up for him and they'll say I'm the violent one. They'll get custody of the boys. I know better than that, but I'm not afraid of him. He'd be in the hospital for a long time."

He imagined how the bastard would look, lying on the ground senseless, ripped open and bleeding, Linda looking at him with astonishment and respect.

"Jimmy. Jimmy." Lucky was gone. Jimmy tried to pull out of the movie playing in his head. Chad was tapping him on the shoulder looking at him funny. "Heads up. The job's done at Alsco an' the crew's comin' back. Make sure you go through the job box and check everything in. You remember me say-in' we might git that big order from Langley? It came through, so I'm puttin' all the men from Alsco on it. It's a rush. Fit 'em out an' make sure they sign for everything."

The droning sound faded and Jimmy nodded. Chad handed him a list of the materials they would need to build the order. "Call and order the steel, then Korn can start pickin' it up tomorrow mornin'."

Jimmy arrived ten minutes early, punched his time card, and went to the supply room where Pop Korn was already waiting at the door. He removed the padlock and Korn followed him inside.

Korn let lose a torrent of frustration. "Dem motha fuggin' directions was all fugged up. You sent me off da wrong exit 'bout five miles da wrong way. I had ta call tha foreman an' he come out an' got me. Lost a hour in da traffic."

"The foreman gave them to me. So what time did you get there?"

"'Bout one." He held out a shopping bag. "Hey, you want some squash? There's more 'an I can eat."

"Sure. You got a garden?"

"A big one. Got ta grow some my own food ta afford de mortgage payments. Got everything paid off 'cept da house."

"Keep scrimping and saving there, Korn."

"Could retire next year, but I ain't."

The Alsco crew started arriving. A pickup drove through the bay doors. Two men got out and unloaded a large box and half a dozen block and tackles with chains. Jimmy counted them and hung them in a steel closet outside his office. Each set weighed eighty pounds. By the time he hung up the last one his arms were swollen from the exertion, making his large forearms look bigger.

He returned to his office and called in orders. One of the Alsco crew walked in, someone he hadn't seen before. A huge figure stood over him, cutting off the air from the fan. "Hey, I'm Mike." Mike stuck out an enormous hand that swallowed Jimmy's. "Most people call me Big Man."

"I'm Jimmy." He wasn't sure what to call him. *Big Man* seemed like a term of submission. He would hate saying it. Yet it was a fact that he was big. He stood at 6'10" and weighed at least 300 pounds by Jimmy's reckoning. He wasn't ripped like a college boy with showy muscles from the gym. It was pure blue collar gristle.

The giant noticed Jimmy's moment of indecision. He was used to that kind of reaction.

"They just say that because I am."

"What do you need?" His Popeye the Sailor forearms shriveled.

"Ten of the .038 rods."

Jimmy pointed to a shelf stacked with bins of welding rods. Big Man picked out ten of what he wanted, five in each hand, then started for the door.

"Hey, everybody's got to sign for parts and write the job number on the sign out sheet," said Jimmy, holding up the form.

"Where's the job number?"

"On the board outside the main office."

"I'll give it to you later."

Jimmy motioned to his desk. "I'll keep the rods, you get the number first."

"Fuck you, ya little faggot." Big Man walked calmly toward the door, rods in hand.

Jimmy shot up from his seat. "Sure, like hell you will."

"Sign this," he said, pointing to his crotch.

"What kind of attitude is that? You're talkin' like a big asshole."

Big Man smirked. As he turned to leave his chest swelled out and his neck muscles corded. "If I want any shit out of you, I'll just squeeze yer head 'till it comes out yer ears."

The pace at the plant quickened and the din of the machines swelled in volume as the days went by. Jimmy ordered more earplugs. Deliveries doubled. Traffic was forced to halt on the main road outside the plant as tractor-trailers maneuvered through the narrow entrance to the yard. Jimmy was constantly directing them in, trying to find space so the forklifts could squeeze alongside and unload.

By the end of the week the yard was filled with beams and pipes. The men had difficulty maneuvering the lengthier pieces into the building. Once inside, they were cut, ground and welded together. The floor became littered with rolling fragments of pipe.

Stairways for Langley were assembled in the back of the plant. Big Man carried a flight of stairs he was working on to a table near the front doors to be cut and welded. He tossed it down as though it was a piece of cardboard and started on it with a disk cutter, sending sparks twelve feet through the air. The arc welder he was working with clamped on the ground wire and began welding step plates to the risers.

"My ole lady said she wanted to move, she couldn't stand it anymore in our apartment," Big Man said. "I threw the sofa through the living room window."

The welder raised his face shield. "Why'd you do that?"

"She said she wanted to move so I moved her." He inserted a bracket into a slit he had cut in a mounting plate to be welded.

The welder attached the grounding clamp to the plate. "What'd she do then?"

"She said she was callin' the cops, so I said, you do and you're goin' through next."

"Jesus. You're crazy."

Big Man grinned. "Maybe."

At midday a flatbed drove in with the last load of materials for the Langley project. It was 100 degrees and waves of heat reflected from the steel bed and the beams piled upon it. Jimmy drove the Heister lift out to the truck. He maneuvered carefully to get close to the bed and had to pull back and aim the forks precisely to get under a big girder. When he started lifting, it locked into the rest of the stack and slipped off the forks. He tilted the forks at more of an angle, then moved forward for a second try. The thousand-pound girder groaned like a prehistoric monster but wouldn't raise.

Big Man had been waiting with the electric lift to bring in some beams on the other side of the truck, but Jimmy was blocking the way. He jumped off and walked alongside Jimmy. "Don't take all day, motherfucker. I got work to do. Do I gotta teach you how to drive that thing?"

"I forgot more about driven' a lift then you'll ever know, mothafucka," Jimmy fleered. He drove the forks in further to get the beam securely balanced.

Big Man shouted in his ear. "Tilt it back motherfucker! Come on up motherfucker, up. Right motherfucker, back motherfucker."

Every time he shouted motherfucker, Jimmy yelled, You're an asshole.

Pop Korn watched the show from the bay door. After the empty truck drove off, Jimmy parked the lift and walked over to him. "I've been a shipping manager for years. I unloaded every kind of rig there is. I unloaded fuckin' bombs. Who the hell does he think he is?"

Pop Korn took off his cap and scratched his head. "That's how he is. He don't know no different."

"He's a big asshole."

"Best to let it go."

"That ain't in me. If I don't give it back, he won't respect me."

Korn put his cap back on. "He is what he is."

The Langley project was the top priority of Wilson Industrial Supply. Hopes for future orders from the government compelled them to complete it on time. By the following Friday stacks of roof girders and neatly numbered fireproof stairways were arranged along the length of the building with the paint still drying.

As the men punched their time cards on Monday morning, Chad told Queball and Lucky to bring the trucks to the front yard for loading the Langley order. Chad turned to Pop Korn. "You're gonna drive the longbed, but the other two trucks gotta get loaded first. Jimmy and Big Man, you're gonna load. Korn, you bring the flatbed up when there's room and give 'em a hand." The men nodded in agreement.

Jimmy went inside the plant but returned shortly. "The only lift that's working is the Heister. The electric and the other two are dead."

Chad spit. "Damnit. That's jist perfect. I'll take a look."

A few minutes later Big Man drove the Heister out through the front bay doors carrying a stairway. He brought it up over the truck bed and lowered it down, then returned several more times, depositing the stairways one at a time. With only one lift they would be late.

The first two trucks were loaded and moved out of the way, then Pop Korn brought the flatbed in. Big Man loaded the twenty-foot roof girders. Korn oversaw the placement and balancing, directing the crew to keep layering the beams with 2 x 4s just ahead of the fork lift.

The last piece was a twelve-hundred-pound steel beam with braces welded on. Big Man got the fork tips under and raised it up high. He drove forward cautiously, positioning the beam over the edge of the truck bed before lowering it down.

Pop Korn shouted over the noise of the engine: "I cain't git da muddafuggin' lanyard on. Come back a foot."

Big Man reversed as Korn moved between the lift and truck bed, signaling to tilt the forks back. It sounded like a gunshot when a pipe stub on the ground punctured the worn front tire. The weight of the beam pushed the piece of pipe through like a cookie cutter through dough. It flattened instantly. The wheel rim spun inside the tire, which overheated and smoked. The lift jerked to the right, causing the beam to slip off the tips of the forks. Pop Korn fell backwards to the ground, his back braced against the wheels.

"Stop, God damnit, stop!" yelled Queball.

Korn stared at the dark stains spreading silently up his pant legs above the beam pinning his ankles.

Big Man shut off the engine and leapt to the end of the beam. Queball and Lucky grabbed on with him, pulling together.

Chad came running with a pike and pried up the end in unison with the other three. "Jimmy. Come on, pull him out. Where the fuck is Jimmy?"

"Let me take the pike," said Big Man. "You pull him out."

"You sure?' said Chad. Released of the weight, he let go and dragged Korn away.

By the time the ambulance arrived, everyone in the plant was gathered in the yard. The medics lifted Korn onto a gurney as a car skidded to a stop blasting its horn. Jimmy stood in the road beneath Liz's billboard talking to himself.

"Jimmy," yelled Chad. "What ya' do'in over there?" Jimmy didn't seem to hear.

Chad motioned everyone back inside. "What are you all lookin' at? Don't stand there gawkin."

It took all day Tuesday to get the lifts fixed and finish loading. Wednesday morning they drove in a convoy to Langley Airfield two days behind schedule. When the yard was free of trucks, Chad hooked up a hose. He turned on the spigot and began washing Korn's blood off the concrete.

Lucky followed behind him with a broom. "That old dude had a lot of blood in him. How do you think his legs are?""

Chad shook his head. "Looks like early retirement. He's gonna get fifty thousand a foot."

"That really sucks."

Chad twisted the nozzle shut. "They transferred Jimmy to a long-term care facility. I want you to fill in for 'im."

"What's wrong with him?"

"I can't even pronounce it. I think it means they don't know."

Quantum Angel

There's a bowing of the trusses overhead as a car slows to a stop. I get off my perch on the strut beneath and look over the railing. A girl, barely eighteen, gets out and shuffles to where I'm watching but doesn't see me. She's a jumper. The stars shine brightly through the cold air of early morning. I feel the fullness of infinity in their radiance. She sees only the darkness between them. She's sown rocks into her coat pockets and will not change her mind. She leans forward over the edge of the bridge with an empty look on her face and I call to her despite knowing she can't see or hear me. No one ever knows I'm there. Then she looks down through me. This will be hard.

What am I doing on the bridge? I'm not Clarence Odbody, if that's what you're wondering. This isn't *It's a Wonderful Life.* Am I invisible? To the eye, yes. But I am here, and an angel may be the closest word that bears semblance to me. With wings? I don't want to even go there. Truth grows dimmer in the constriction of words. Words distract.

I'll do my best to explain. I'll start with a question: "What is the Void?" To many the word means *empty.* But it is not. The Void is not empty, but infinite: neither dark, light, cold, hot, large, nor small, not any one thing, but everything. It's an infinity of possibilities without constrictions; a fullness of creation that spills over into the existence of our lives: a miracle. A nonlinear multiverse. It's where I come from.

You could think of me as a being of the multiverse. And why perch under a bridge? Back to the Void. In the Void are infinite realities. Not universes but multiverses with suns and planets, life and history. Each with its own time, consequences and outcomes. It's quantum physics without the physics. Who but The Creator could conceive of this vastness? I'm a servant, a tool to the vastness of infinity. That's why I am under the bridge. The concrete and beams are finite and comfort me. It's a place to start from and come back to.

You may wonder how anybody can live under a bridge. I don't have a body. No arms, no legs. I have sentience, but not a heart that beats like yours. I'm an intermediary between your world and the Void where I come from. In that other place are planes of existence; other dimensions and realities. I look into it and see them like you see a table or chair on the floor. It's an extra sense, like a whale's sonar sensing mass, or a dog sniffing your leg and knowing who you've been with or where you've been for the last three days.

Do you think you are in one place at a specific point in time? Are you standing on a bridge, about to jump, or reading a book at your desk? There are other planes in the infinity of the Void, and I can take you and bring you into any one of them that I choose. That's my power. I'm a quantum angel, and I can take you from one plane of existence and put you into another. You will be transformed.

When you lay a silk cloth down upon a table a ripple travels to the edge as it lands. A pocket of air causes the ripple as it escapes, then the cloth flattens and the wrinkle is gone. That's what the transformation is like: soft and smooth; cushioned on air; undetectable. And when you are done, the wrinkles are gone. When someone jumps from my bridge, I transform them. If you jump from my bridge, I'll take you.

Her name is Laura. She is falling now to the river below. She's half way down. Now half of that half, then half again and again, falling through the multiverse. I feel her electricity and reach to take her. As I pull her in, I enter her mind. There is a weight there that is heavier than the stones in her pockets and I quickly scan through her memories. Where does the unraveling start?

The synapses and axons of her being snap with electricity. I inhale the pungent ozone, following the trail of current like a dog on the scent. We're moving in the space between two thoughts. Between half of that space, and half of that, again and again.

She has left the trail, and from here I'll take her and put her in another plane, a plane with no wrinkles; a better place. There is the wrinkle:

Her mother takes a beer out of the refrigerator and lights a cigarette. She shouts at Laura from the kitchen. "Get up. You can't stay in bed all day."

"I had to work late."

"Don't give me any damn mouth." Laura throws on her clothes and hurries past the kitchen to the front door unnoticed. Her mother picks up the phone and starts yelling into the smoke yellow mouthpiece at her boyfriend.

Laura hurries into class late, feeling self-conscious as the other students turn their heads and watch her walk to her desk. The faded flowers and sweat stains under the armpits of her old blouse seem to stand out more with each step. The sweat stains expand and soak downward. She imagines herself giving off a scent that the others smell across the room.

When she gets home the TV is blaring and her mother is passed out on the couch ...

The river churns below. The stars shine above the bridge, spinning in infinity. I see myself on other worlds looking back with infinite variation in unending permutations; world after world. The Void opens and I enter.

There is no up, down, or sideways. The planes of infinite realities stretch forever in all directions. Where is the right place for her, the one without the wrinkle? On one world, she lives in another country. In another is a reality without rivers and bridges. Can I find the perfect place to put her? I do the best I can.

The search is hard, but I see it. I take her electricity, her being, and enfold it in a fine silk cloth, transporting her to the new place I've found. We arrive in her bedroom at her bed, and I lay the cloth down. It floats softly and spreads out. The ripple moves to the edge and flattens.

Laura breaths deeply from the air of her new world and jumps out of bed. She walks into the kitchen. "How many pancakes do you want?" her mother asks.

My charge is complete. The worlds recede in a flash of blue-violet light. The portal closes. I'm back at my perch beneath the empty bridge. The concrete and beams are finite and comfort me.

Thumb Tacks

We moved to Stamford, Connecticut, the month before West Side Story came out in October 1961. In Stamford I learned how to survive school. During the school day cherry bombs blew toilets into bits. You were expected to belong to a gang. A self-imposed dress code of all black included pointed shoes with cleats. I put thumb tacks in my heels. Stiletto knives were a forbidden necessity if you wanted to be somebody. Mom bought me a Boy Scout knife at the department store, refusing to let me have the switchblade on the next shelf. Rumbling in town and who you knew were bragging points. My best friend, Donald Mazola, could have passed for thirty and was built like a linebacker. We were a gang of two but preferred listening to 45 records and reading science fiction.

I rode the same bus Frank Fischer rode. Frank was at the top of the hood chain. On the first day of school I got on the bus behind another kid my age and height. The bus was full except for a torn-up seat at the back. The kid took the spot next to the window and I sat next to him.

Someone tapped me from behind. "You don't want to sit there."

I turned and gave him a look. "Why not?"

"That's Frank Fischer's seat."

"So. Who's Frank Fischer?"

He snickered. No one was at the next stop, but the driver kept open the door while cold air poured in. A tall teenager with sunken cheeks and a scar down the side of his face swaggered up to the bus from three houses down the street, both arms swinging in the same direction hood style. "Thanks, Bill."

"Sure, Frank." Bill pulled the door closed and gave him time to make his way to the back. Frank stared into my face as he dragged his cleats over the floor. I got up and forced myself into the back row as the bus started forward. Frank stood over his seat, flicked out the blade of his stiletto and slashed the back of the seat next to the intruder who sat there frozen. "This is *my* seat." The kid got up and Frank backhanded him, then let him slide by into the aisle. The kid lurched his way to the front and held on to the door-well pole, beet faced all the way to school. Frank plunked down on his seat and stabbed more holes into the cushion.

"I told them it was your seat, Frank," the boy who tapped me on the shoulder said. Sycophants all, we rode in terror for another month until Frank Fischer, already three years behind, pulled the fire alarm and graduated to reform school.

Dad got transferred to Princeton, New Jersey, the next fall. I borrowed his pliers and happily pulled the remnants of thumbtacks from my shoes.

Hard Cider

No sooner had The Beatles appeared on the Ed Sullivan Show in February of 1964, then my family was off to England. Our move from Pennsylvania was complicated by a shipyard crane dropping the shipping container holding our furniture. My mother turned it into an opportunity to replace the bent and broken things with English antiques acquired at auctions. The English set the bar for an antique to be four hundred years old or more. She was able to get bargains on two-hundred-year-old grandfather clocks, tables and chairs, dinnerware, and crystal that were sought after in The States where it was difficult to find things over a hundred.

We house hunted in London, but the homes were gloomy and smelled like cabbage. Finding schooling was difficult. Canes of various thickness stood racked outside the headmasters' offices. It was not reassuring to hear that canes were hardly ever used anymore. The English schools would not allow me to enter the British education system. By the tenth grade American public schools were two years behind the English. The British students were preparing for O and A level exams and on a path to university or trade education. My younger sister, Lydia, and brother, Jeff, were not yet beyond hope and were accepted.

My parents fell in love with an eighteenth-century manor in Sundridge, near Sevenoaks, Kent. It was called Greystone Court and was divided into three separate homes. Greystones was approached from a single driveway leading to three separate courtyards in the back. The front was kept in its original state facing the beautiful Kent countryside. Our third of the manor had a huge expanse of lawn, a gazebo, and a sunken rose garden. A solarium opened onto a wide veranda overlooking hedged gravel paths. In America it was my job to cut the grass and rake the leaves, but I could not get the English lawnmower to start. There was a flame thrower to control the weeds which I managed to ignite. It incinerated half the main path but fizzled out and I never could get it going again. We let the weeds grow until forced to hire a gardener.

The living room was used to entertain Mom and Dad's friends and business associates. It had a sunken floor with an ornate fireplace and French doors opening out to the veranda. The bedrooms were on the second floor and we were one short. I was assigned the library on the third floor for my bedroom. The walls were lined with English history, mysteries, and contemporary literature, including the unexpurgated version of *Lady Chatterley's Lover* banned in the United States.

New Beacon Boys School in Sevenoaks took my brother in. He did well and got good at soccer. "What do they say about losing the Revolutionary War?" I asked one day.

He cracked a grin. "They had to let us go because they were too busy ruling the world."

Lydia enrolled in Combe Bank Convent where nuns daily smacked the students' knuckles with rulers and dealt verbal blows. Before her first year ended, she and three other girls hopped on a double decker bus outside the school entrance and made it halfway to London before the nuns caught up with them and hauled them back. They nearly got away. All were placed on disciplinary probation. I am proud of her for being the ringleader of the rebellion. Dad was, too. She was a leader.

Far into the school year it was decided the best solution for me was a boarding school in Bury St. Edmunds, Suffolk, called Herringswell Manor International School. Boys were required to wear a blazer, tie, smart trousers, and leather shoes; girls a blazer, white blouse, skirt below the knees, and calf socks. No sneakers or dungarees.

The Sunday before I was due to leave, I convinced my parents I was old enough to buy my clothes myself. They gave me the money to shop in London at Selfridges. But this was the era of Swinging London, so I made my way to Carnaby Street instead and bought a double-breasted Edwardian pinstripe blazer and matching bell bottoms, a flowered shirt and paisley tie. And a pair of leather Mod boots with high heels. Technically it was a suit – and the boots were leather.

When I got back home in the evening Mom was upset. It was my first *you-did-what?* "Whatever possessed you to do such a thing? Your father will be furious. It's a good thing he isn't here right now." I imagined Dad's eyes bulging out of their sockets, but he had already left for the airport.

Mom was willing to play it by ear. I wore my Carnaby Street suit as we headed out to Herringswell Manor by train on Monday morning. Built in the early 1900s, the estate had been acquired by two partners with ambitions to establish it as an international school catering to Canadians and Americans: an Irishman named McDermott and a retired American colonel named Villiers. Mr. McDermott greeted us at the entrance and gave us a tour. For all the mock-Tudor grandeur of the outside, the interior of the main house was austere and pervaded by a damp chill. Once white walls were tinted with age and the dark-stained woodwork plain. The snooker table in the pool room looked promising but the turn of the century easy chairs sagged to the floor. Cue stick racks lined walls covered in scuffed wrought leather. The girls dorm was on the second floor, off limits to the boys. Mr. McDermott showed the classrooms and the lounge, then drove us over to the boys residence hall.

The house was split in two. One side was the domicile of the dorm parents, the Andrasanins. Mr. Andrasanin was also the biology teacher. In the lounge, the smell of curry comingled with the odor of burning coal from the fireplace.

Mom gave me a brave smile. "I'll send you a hot plate and some cans of stew."

"Sorry, hotplates aren't allowed. Biscuits and chocolate are fine, though," said Mr. McDermott.

The boy students' rooms lined the hallway spanning the second floor. There were two beds to a room with a coal fireplace between. In the bathroom was a clawfoot tub with a water heater mounted above on the wall. The bathroom was heated by an electric space heater. I could see my breath in the air. Mr. McDermott led me to my room and explained the rules: smoking was allowed but use the ashtrays, no alcohol, curfew at 10 p.m. Supper was at 5:30. It was here my mother took her leave. They left me to unpack.

I laid my suitcase on the bed closest to the fireplace. As I hung up my clothes my roommate walked in, a short wiry fellow with a beard and curly hair. He introduced himself as Jon Rauss and told me I was on his bed, but to take my time. Jon pulled a pack of Gauloise from his shirt pocket and offered me one.

"They're strong," he said, watching with interest as I inhaled.

I nodded, trying to control my choking. "Where are you from?"

"Switzerland. I have dual citizenship with the U.S., actually."

"Why did you pick this school?"

Jon shrugged. "My parents picked it. I got expelled from Lausanne for drinking." He took a deep drag and propelled the lungful across the room in perfect rings. "What does your dad do?"

"He works for World Trade Corporation. He's in marketing."

"My dad is John D. Rockefeller's lawyer. Winnie Rockefeller is my best friend. I'm flying to New York next weekend to see him so you'll have the room to yourself." I couldn't top that.

We assembled in the main lounge of the manor house in the morning to wait for breakfast. I walked in with Jon and he introduced me. Seven boys and seven girls made up the student body. I was number fifteen. I found a warm spot by the fire and lit a Players, trying to fit in. The others were dressed according to code in clothes from shops on Saville Row and shirts hand stitched in Hong Kong. At least I was the tallest in my high heeled boots.

A few weeks later I had settled-in to the school routine properly dressed in a two-button blazer, charcoal pants, and black Oxford shoes. English and biology became my favorite subjects, largely due to the lack of textbooks. Creative writing exercises helped me develop my imagination to write fiction and didn't require a textbook. Drawing specimens from the Linnaeus classification system was interesting despite not being able to understand what Mr. Andrasanin was saying.

Colonel Villiers played the role of physical education teacher and conducted class in a raggedy sweat suit from his military days. He led us on runs about the grounds, then lined us up to shoot hoops on the concrete driveway of one of the outbuildings. I wasn't good at basketball and made the mistake of getting in his way, bouncing off him as though he was a brick wall. Get up, moon child, he ordered. I got up and took a shot, missing by a mile.

The weeks turned into months. To pass the time after supper we played pop tunes and lip synched to The Spencer Davis Group, Neil

Diamond, The Hollies and The Yardbirds. The winter wore on and the short breads and chocolates from home no longer took the edge off the tasteless boarding school diet. The rumblings in our stomachs were accompanied by grumbling. One evening we decided we had enough.

"There's a pub half a mile down the road," said Jon. "They have fish and chips."

Larry always talked about the cookouts back home in Oregon. "A steak would be nice."

"I've lost eight pounds," I chimed in.

"You up for it," Larry asked.

"Don't look at me."

"Since nobody's volunteering, how about drawing straws?" Larry pulled a box of wooden matches from his pants pocket and broke the end of one. He handed the bunch to Jon. "You do it. Shuffle them."

Jon lined up the heads and held them out in his fist. Mine was the short match. "Okay, I'll go."

"Get some beer, too," said Jon.

Everyone put in a couple of pounds and I stuffed the notes in my pocket. I turned off the outside lights and closed the front door slowly behind me to avoid creaking it, but instead it let out a long, throbbing, groan. I looked over to the door leading into the Andrasanins' apartment. All clear. Fifteen minutes later I walked up to the bar of the Whitehart Tuddenham.

"We can't serve you," said the bartender.

I could barely pass for sixteen let alone eighteen. "Do you serve fish and chips?"

"We're fresh out."

I didn't give up. "I'm from the school down the road. The food's really bad." I pointed at the meat pies on the bar. "Can you sell me those?"

"What the bloody fuck." He motioned with his head. "Walk around outside and meet me at the back door."

It was several minutes until the door opened. "Best I can do, mate." He handed me a box of meat pies and a bag with three bottles of hard cider. I fished out the wad of money from my pocket and handed it to him. "Ta," he said and closed the door. I rapped impatiently.

The door opened a crack. "What now?"

"What about my change?"

"Is that the thanks I get? Piss off. Consider yourself fortunate."

When I got back to the dorm the front door was locked. The lounge was empty. I went to the Andrasanin's side of the building and threw pebbles at Larry's windowpanes above their kitchen window. He opened the sash and leaned out.

"The door's locked," I whispered.

"Climb the trellis."

I looked up at the ivy covering the latticework. "I need two hands to climb."

Several heads appeared near the window and huddled together. A minute later Larry lowered two sheets knotted together. "Tie them in these."

I made the end of one of the sheets into a sling and loaded the contraband. The bottles clanged cheerfully against the side of the building on their hand-over-hand journey upward. I climbed the trellis and scrambled over the sill behind them. We polished off the pies and cider and were deeply satisfied.

The next morning Mr. McDermott called me into his office and pointed to the seat in front of his desk. "You were seen climbing up the side of the building after hours last night. Mr. Andrasanin found cider bottles in the trash. Am I missing something?"

After my full confession I was suspended for two weeks. The train back to Sevenoaks was empty in the middle of the day and clattered noisily over the rails. The familiarity of the passing landscape served as a reminder I was getting closer to home and my father's anger. My anxiety grew.

I lugged the suitcase from the bus stop in Sundridge up the hill to Greystones in a drizzle and was let in dripping by Mrs. Hedges, our housekeeper. Mother was out shopping, so I went upstairs and unpacked my clothes and the notebooks I needed to keep up with schoolwork. Two weeks banishment is a lot of time, but on the shelf over the desk was the means of escape: *Ape and Essence, Catcher in the Rye,* and *Lady Chatterley's Lover;* the uncensored, uncut version.

Mothers of murdering sons sentenced to hang have countless times pleaded the innocence of their child, yet I was uncertain of the outcome. All the bad stuff in my whole life added together could not hold a candle to getting suspended. I told Mom the entire saga over roast beef sandwiches and tea when she got home.

It turned out Dad was in the Hague for another two weeks, so there was a reprieve. She listened patiently as I told my side of the story. "Mr. McDermott called me this morning to let me know you were suspended. Now that you told me about the food situation, I'm giving him a piece of my mind. All the money we pay them . . . if they fed you better none of this would have happened."

Mr. McDermott confessed it was Colonel Villiers who wanted to expel me permanently, but he had argued for a three-day suspension. Two weeks was the compromise, but he could not change that. He agreed to talk to the cook. My humiliation was over.

Mother was busy shopping for antiques during most of the time of my exile and I was on my own. An old Lambretta motor scooter that wouldn't start was tucked under a tarp in a corner of the courtyard. Mrs. Hedges's son, Charles, took me on a bicycle tour of Sundridge and showed me a garage that stocked scooter parts. With a new spark plug and carburetor float it sprang to life and I was able to take scooter rides on the back roads.

Most of the time I had the place to myself and did a lot of reading. My library bedroom had French-style windows that open outward to the steep hip roofs of the manor. To the left, it was all twelve-pitch terracotta. To the right, you could see the front lawn three stories below and tiny cattle grazing in the distance.

The end of the first week I finished *Catcher in the Rye* and was halfway into *Lady Chatterley's Lover*. It was 27 degrees Celsius (eighty-one degrees Fahrenheit,) unusually warm, and I opened the window. I like to read in bed and flopped down, returning to my place, the part where the lover is stripped to the waist and washing himself while Lady Chatterley is watching. I continued reading for all the wrong reasons. There was a tapping on the windowpane.

"Hello. Do you mind if I pop in?"

Startled, I look across the room. In the window, with the sunlight pouring in, is a brown-haired girl my own age crouching on her haunches on the sill. She wears a dark pair of tights and blouse.

Before I can answer she hops to the floor. "I'm your neighbor. I live next door in the middle."

I'm reminded of her strong resemblance to Emma Peel from the Avengers. Not sure if she is real, I slide from the bed and stand there facing her, wondering what to say.

"Did you walk here over the roof?" We don't shake hands.

"Along the gutter, actually. You're a Yank, aren't you?" *Like, don't you ever walk three stories up along the gutter, too?* Her eyes rest on the can of Three Nuns pipe tobacco on the desk and she smiles. "Are you on holiday?"

I dig for something to impress her and panic. At first, absolute dead air nothingness, then decide to play the victim. "I was suspended from school for drinking – hard cider."

"For that? How awful."

Names are exchanged. Hers is Amanda. It turns out she was let out of her school early to attend a funeral that afternoon. "I must get back before they notice I'm gone. It was really nice meeting you, Tom." She hops back on the sill and steps catlike onto the roof, smiling. "Cheerio."

Early the next morning I played Beatle songs downstairs in the living room on our grand piano. With the top up, real loud. Halfway through "I Want to Tell You" the phone rings. "Yes, hello, I'm your neighbor. I hope you don't mind me asking, but do you like The Beatles?"

He hadn't given his name. It seemed he must be complaining about playing too loud so early in the morning. "I apologize. It's much too early."

"Oh, not at all. Good choice, I enjoyed it. Do you mind if I ask, but how old are you?"

"Seventeen."

"I am so happy The Beatles caught on with you Americans. So glad we had this chance to chat. I won't disturb you any longer. Goodbye."

The phone clicked. *How polite.* I never saw his daughter again.

Paphiopedilum

T he salesman twisted off the cap of his pen and dipped the nib in ink before handing it over. "Just squeeze it in right there. Your full signature."

It was more than he wanted to spend. Mitchell took a deep breath and wrote in a scratchy hand: Mitchell A. Tubbs.

"Swell. You're now the owner of a 1923 Oldsmobile Model 30A, the finest car on the road. We'll need to get the paper work started for your operator's license." He laid the application form on the desk.

"I'll apply later."

"It's the new regulation. You got to have a driver's license to take it out on the road. Fill out the application and I'll deliver the car to your home after it's prepped."

Mitchell nodded. "Guess I don't have a choice." He glanced up at the clock over the desk and knew he would be late for dinner.

After a handshake, he race walked to the trolley stop on the corner of Kensington and the Boulevard and made it in time to jump through the open door for the pole. He pulled himself inside and found a seat as it whirred up to speed. Further down Kensington the tram made a stop and the refrain from a popular tune came through the half open window:

"Gee, but it's hard to love someone when that someone don't love you! I'm so disgusted, heart-broken, too; I've got those down-hearted blues..." (From Down Hearted Blues lyrics by Alberta Hunter. Popularized by Bessie Smith.)

He thought about the heads that would turn whenever he pulled up in the Olds with Jenny Moore. He was a man on the rise. She was a wow and it was hard to believe she was his. He might even teach her to drive. The electric lines overhead arced making the turn onto Patterson Avenue. *Should he pop the question? Maybe soon. But not tonight.*

He got off at Forest and walked the last two blocks home. As he approached the front steps, she moved away from the window. Jenny took his hat as he walked through the door and planted a kiss on his lips. "Did you have to work late?"

"No, I'm sorry, sugar," said Mitchell. "Applying for the license took longer than I thought. I've got something to tell you, Jenny."

"Oh, Mitchell, honey. You sit down and I'll bring out dinner. I kept it warm. Then you tell me. I've waited so long to hear this."

"You have?"

Her cheeks flushed. "Yes."

Jenny disappeared into the kitchen, then returned with two plates of food that she had kept warm on the stove. She sat across from Mitchell and scooched the chair to the table, being careful not to press the swell of her stomach into the edge. Reaching across, she placed her hand on his and looked into his eyes. "Now, what is it you want to say to me?"

In the back of Mitchell's mind there was an ethereal impression that things were going too well. "I stopped to apply for a license after work. I can apply for one for you, too. If you want."

She laughed. "You silly man, don't you know how it works? A license is for both of us."

An alarm bell rang inside his head. "It's the new law they passed. You have to have a registration and license when you buy a car now. I bought an Oldsmobile. Wait till you see it. It's green with brown leather seats, and it's got a twenty horsepower engine. You're going to love it."

Her lips quivered. "You didn't apply for a marriage license?"

"Honey pie, you know we'll get married, but not this second, not just like that."

"Well then, when?"

When? He was going to pop the question on his terms. When he was ready.

Her fingers paradiddled the table. "Do you love me?"

"Positively," he replied.

"Are we going to get married?"

"Absolutely, positively, but not just now."

Jenny's fist smote the side of her plate, catapulting her dinner across the room. She stood, knocked over her chair, then heaved with sobs.

Mitchell sat dumbfounded. Yelling was hard to deal with, but the tears worse. "Sugar, don't. Will you ma mar ... ? Will you, will you ... ?"

Her shoulders stopped heaving. "What?"

"Shoot. You know we will."

"You don't love me. I wouldn't marry you now for all the money on earth. I don't ever want to be Mrs. Tubbs." She heaved a cup at Mitchell's head. "Get out of my sight!"

As the cup came flying he realized he was unsure he loved her. Not like the way he knew he wanted that Oldsmobile. *Spend the rest of my life living with this hellion wild woman?* "You are a hellion!"

Jenny pointed to the door. "Go. Leave."

"This is my house," yelled Mitchell. The walls shook as the door slammed behind him.

Too angry to pay attention to where he was going, he recognized the entrance to Cheswick Park and entered. They had shared intimate moments along the winding paths before. Mitchell kept walking to calm himself down, but he couldn't get a handle on the contumely that had just happened. He realized he was in the middle of the woods. The path had deteriorated into a barely discernible trail that was difficult to follow. He couldn't see the opening where he entered, or the picnic tables either. It seemed that if he kept going in the same direction, he should come out on the street behind the park called Alvarado Road.

He came out of the woods on a deserted lane that was not the Alvarado he knew and walked toward the sun, low in the West. Rounding a bend, he noticed a heavy soporific odor. It was like a perfume, but so powerful it made him feel sleepy. The fragrance continued to intensify as he came upon a cedar-shingled Cape Cod set back from the road. A flagstone path meandered to the edge of the lawn. Along the border of the lawn was a beautiful garden. A neatly lettered sign read: MADAM HEL, CRYSTALLOMANCY.

A regal looking woman kneeling in the garden rose and looked him up and down. It seemed to Mitchell that she must be someone famous or descended from a noble family. Although she was advanced in years, her face held a vitality and strength that he had never seen in a woman before. Shining white hair fell straight to her shoulders. The nose and chin were perfectly formed, and a single eye held a penetrating intelligence. The other was covered by a patch.

She spoke with a touch of detached humor. "So, what is your opinion of my garden?"

"I've never seen flowers like these." He looked down into the bed to break away from her gaze. Each flower was a unique combination of coruscating color with a personality of its own. The crests looked like little beards. "What are they?"

"A strain I developed myself. Paphiopedilum abbatis quiesco."

"They're beautiful."

"But not this one." She pointed with her trowel to one that was drooping. In one deft motion she knelt, enucleated the sickly spawn, reached beneath the soil, then pulled it up with the bulb in the palm of her hand. The bulb, the size of a fist, rippled like a beating heart. She dropped it in a burlap sack. "Weed. The trowel must do its work. You can't let the bad seed in."

"I have to be getting home," he replied nervously.

"Don't go. Let me tell your fortune."

"No thank you, ma'am."

"Let me see your hand." She took his hand and turned the palm up. Mitchell felt sluggish. The heavy, sweet smell slowed his responses. She traced the lines of his palm with her finger. "I see some long lines and some short lines. I see you're worried about a girl. She has upset you. You want to know what to do."

He didn't resist. "That's right."

"You want to know what to do about ..." She studied his face. "Jenny."

"How did you know her name?"

"I can tell you more." She smiled. "Are you sure you don't want to know your fortune?"

"How much does it cost?"

"The first time is free."

He pulled his hand away. "I can't argue about the price."

"Then we're agreed. Let's go out back to the gazebo. It's very quiet there." She led him around the side of the house. The odiferous scent grew stronger as they followed the walk through an expanse of lawn that was the canvas of an artist, one who had used tulip trees, rose of Sharon, and mistletoe, as paint. Paphiopedilum were clustered in each hollow at every turn. In the epicenter of this visual feast was an intricate maze with a gazebo.

She led him to an opening in the maze. "Don't let go of my hand. It's hard to find the way through."

He followed obediently. After winding through the green labyrinth, they stepped onto the floor of the gazebo. A massive oak table with a crystal ball sat at the center.

Madam Hel pointed to one of two chairs for him to sit at and followed suit in the other. "Shall we begin?"

Mitchell nodded. He looked into the crystal, at first seeing only the underside of the gazebo roof reflected in the polished surface. Then clouds formed within the ball. They churned, swirled, and separated, revealing him and Jenny at the dinner table. The crystallomancer's translucent face floated before him in the glass. The crystal distorted the eyepatch, making it larger.

"I see a table. You and Jenny are quarreling."

"We did quarrel."

Madam Hel's face continued to float in the crystal, but the patch continued to expand. It seemed to squirm from underneath.

He looked up from the crystal, focusing on her patch. Something was pushing from underneath.

"You're staring," she said. "Don't stare."

He gaped. "No ma'am. I'm not."

"Yes, you are. You are a bad boy, Mitchell. You're rude to me, and you are rude to Jenny."

"How do you know my name?"

She ignored him and began to shake, slowly at first, then faster. In a moment her entire body shook with convulsive trembling. She slumped downward and raised her arms, then spoke in Jenny's voice:

"Do you love me?"

"Absolutely," Mitchell heard himself say.

"Are you going to marry me?" asked the Jenny voice.

"Absolutely, positively, just not now," Mitchell whispered. "I have to go."

Madam Hel crushed his hand in hers. An electric surge flowed into Mitchell. His free hand extended upward from the galvanic charge and raised into the air. He twisted to free himself. "Let go of me, witch."

"You don't know to whom you are speaking, boy."

"Let go," he repeated, unable to pull away.

"You have two futures. The one in the crystal with Jenny, or the one in here." She pointed at her patch.

"Please, let me go."

"If I did, you wouldn't be able to find your way out of here. No one has. I'm tired of arguing. You've made your choice." She pulled the patch from her eye with her free hand and drew Mitchell closer with the other, turning her head to bring the exposed socket in which rested an engorged white walnut rimmed with yellow custard directly in front of his face. Swollen vessels ran from the necrotic eye's rim into the black hole of the center. The strange fragrance and electric current held him in place, paralyzed. "Welcome to your future."

The hole locked onto Mitchell. It dilated and he felt a pull. The hole widened and the light in the garden faded. It continued to grow and envelope him. He began descending into a well with no bottom. As he fell, he felt himself dissolving into the blackness.

"Let me go witch, let me go." He faded until there was not a soul fragment remaining.

She let go of his hand and removed the trowel from a pocket in her dress. Her other hand clamped his shoulder, and in a series of deft strokes, she incised about his heart and extracted it, hot and beating.

He was in the blackness for what seemed an eternity, then a rising upward began. There was stretching, a growing longer, then a patch of light. Grainy and distorted at first, it grew brighter and clearer.

"There you are." Madam Hel loomed overhead. "Welcome, my Paphiopedilum."

He bobbed in the wind. He had no mouth and could not answer.

Jenny reset the table, then stepped back and bit on a nail. She headed out the door in the direction of Cheswick Park wondering if he had been there. There wasn't much to go on, but that was all she could think of.

She hurried through the gates and along the path she and Mitchell had taken before. She thought about her predicament and began sobbing. When she could cry no longer, she dried her eyes and looked through a salty haze into the woods. A trail of broken grass indicated someone had been there before.

Jenny pushed her way through until she emerged on Alvarado Road. As she rounded the bend, she came upon Madam Hel kneeling in her garden. The strong fragrance in the air made her nauseous.

"Are you well, my dear?" asked Madam Hel, rising.

"It will pass," Jenny replied.

"You're upset. You should take up gardening. It has a calming effect."

"Are these orchids?"

"You're such a clever girl. Paphiopedilum abbatis quiesco, my own strain. Let me give you one to take home."

"I couldn't."

Madam Hel held out a flowerpot. "Please. I was about to plant this one but I want you to have it. Give it plenty of water and it will do well."

The flower reminded her of Mitchell. "Did you see a young man come by? Good looking?"

"I know who you mean. I read his fortune, then he left. Take this and forget all about him. You'll find someone better soon, I'm sure."

She had set the flower on the kitchen window sill when the car salesman knocked on the front door. He doffed his straw boater. "I'm Woody Swink from Broad Street Motors. Is Mr. Tubbs in?"

"No. But it looks like he's not coming home for dinner." She smiled coyly and extended her hand. "I'm Jenny, his fiancé. Woody, have you had supper? It would be a shame for the food to go to waste."

"That would be swell."

Starman

Adapted from *Micromegas,* written in 1752 by Voltaire

On a planet of the Dog Star, Sirius, in the constellation Canis Majoris of our own Milky Way, lived a youth with an inquiring mind by the name of Micromegas. In the abundance of the universe he was as his appellation implied: small and big, being somewhere in the middle of things. Whereas we of the blue planet, in the endless variation of nature, tend to reach a height of five or six feet, Micromegas was a colossus by comparison. Not only in stature, but in the number of his senses, intellect, and longevity. The following is a brief summary:

Stature: 120,000 feet tall, 50,000 feet in girth, and 6,333 feet in nose length.

Senses: Over 1,000. Not limited to our own five senses, but including many more such as sonar, infrared, various built-in timers, a Geiger counter, a digital multimeter, a carbon dating organ, a polygraph, and an atomic absorption spectrophotometer. On his forehead, beneath a luxurious shock of hair, was a telencephalonic bump of bone that functioned as a thought receiver and transmitter when in proximity to other thinking beings.

Intellect: He studied at the best university of his planet, discovering many mathematical propositions and a formula which always beat the stock market which he used to pay for his education.

Longevity: Our own Galapagos turtle is but a flash in the pan. He and others of his Sirian kind live well over a thousand years. (Yet they complain that life is too short.)

This would lead us to believe he enjoyed a wonderful life in the best of all possible worlds, but there came a point when, like too many of us, his delusions were shattered. It was his rational, inquiring mind that got him into trouble with the elders of Sirius. In his 450th year, still a mere youth, he wrote a treatise suggesting there was an underlying similarity and oneness to all forms in the universe. He suggested that one form simply gave way to another through the process of life and death, and that this process of re-arrangement was infinite throughout nature. This idea shocked the elders so badly that they exiled him for 800 years. Micromegas was not troubled though, for he thought the elders ignorant and trifling. He decided to improve his mind and further his learning by means of travel, and set out on a journey from planet to planet.

He was glad for an excuse to escape the contumely of his planet and immediately put his vast knowledge of gravity and the forces of repulsion and attraction to work. Enveloping himself in a blanket of his planet's atmosphere, he latched on to the tail of a passing comet and rose above the planet, then entered a sunbeam and streaked away at the speed of light. It was his intention to hop from planet to planet in this manner.

Micromegas wound his way along the starry road, making several turns and swerving often to avoid asteroid belts and to stay clear of an undiscovered wormhole. He arrived at the planet Saturn but was astonished at its smallness of size and the diminutive stature of its inhabitants. Though Saturn is about 900 times the size of Earth and its people six thousand feet high, Micromegas considered it puny and was tempted to look down on them and ridicule them, but being a person of good sense, thought twice about it and had to admit to himself that they may be capable of good intellect. He decided to become familiar with them, and after a period of time, they grew used to his extraordinary appearance. He developed a friendship with the Secretary of the Academy of Saturn, a man who was able to give a good accounting of others and was also a poet and mathematician. One day they struck up a conversation.

THE CONVERSATION BETWEEN MICROMEGAS AND THE INHABITANT OF SATURN

On Sirius it was a matter of politeness not to invade the privacy of others by using their thought reading bumps. They would first ask permission, but Micromegas felt the complexity of explaining this to the secretary, who lacked the ability, would be an obstacle to their communication. The starman laid himself down, and the secretary approached his nose.

"It must be confessed," said Micromegas, pretending to speak with his mouth, "that nature is full of variety."

"Yes," replied the Saturnian, "nature is like a great garden, whose flowers-"

"Faddle! Forget about your gardens."

The secretary smiled bravely. "Like an assembly of fair and dark haired women? Whose dresses-"

"Your brunettes are a vexation to me," said our young traveler.

"Then it is like a gallery of paintings, the brush strokes which-"

"Not at all," answered Micromegas, "No. Nature is like nature, and comparisons are odious."

"Well, to please you," said the secretary, bowing.

"I won't be pleased," replied the Sirian, "I want to be instructed. Begin, therefore, without further preamble, and tell me how many senses the people of this world enjoy."

"We have seventy and two," said the academician, "but we are daily complaining of the small number, as our imagination transcends those that we have been given. With seventy-two senses, our five moons and ring, we find ourselves very much restricted. Notwithstanding our curiosity and the number of passions that result from these few senses, we still have time enough to be tired of idleness."

Micromegas's eyes widened with excitement. "I sincerely believe what you say. Though we Sirians have a thousand different senses, there still remains a vague desire, an unaccountable inquietude incessantly admonishing us of our own unimportance. We have come to understand that there are beings on other worlds who are our superiors in point of perfection. I have traveled a little and seen mortals both above and below myself in the scale of being, but I have not met one who had less desire than necessity, and more want than gratification. Perhaps one day I'll arrive in some country where nothing is wanting, but I have at this time no certain information of such a happy land."

The Saturnian and his guest exhausted themselves in conjectures upon this subject, and after much argumentation equally ingenious and uncertain, wanted to return to concrete facts.

"To what age do you commonly live?" said the Sirian.

The little gentleman shook his head sadly. "A mere trifle."

"It is the very same case with us. The shortness of life is our daily complaint, so that this must be a universal law in nature."

"Alas!" cried the Saturnian. "Few, very few on this globe outlive five hundred great revolutions of the sun. (These, according to our way of reckoning, amount to live about fifteen thousand years.) So, you see, we in a manner begin to die the very moment we are born. Our existence is no more than a point, our duration an instant, and our globe an atom. Scarce do we begin to learn a little, when death intervenes before we can profit by experience. For my own part, I am deterred from laying schemes when I consider myself as a single drop in the midst of an immense ocean. I am particularly ashamed, in your presence, of the ridiculous figure I make among my fellow-creatures."

Micromegas shifted his weight and leaned forward. "If you were not a philosopher, I would be afraid of mortifying your pride by telling you that the term of our lives is seven hundred times longer than yours. However, you must understand that when the texture of the body is resolved, in order to reanimate nature in another form, which is the consequence of what we call death, when that moment of change arrives, there is not the least difference between having lived a whole eternity, or a single day. I have been in countries where the people live a thousand times longer than with us, and yet they murmured at the shortness of their time. But one will find everywhere a few persons of good sense, who know how to make the best of their portion and thank the author of nature for his bounty. There is a profusion of variety scattered through the universe, and yet there is an admirable vein of uniformity that runs through the whole. For example, all thinking beings are different among themselves, though at bottom they resemble one another in the powers and passions of the soul. Matter, though interminable, has different properties in every sphere. So, let me ask you, 'How many principal properties of matter do you have in your world?'"

The Saturnian's brows knitted. "If you mean those properties without which our globe could not subsist, we reckon in all three hundred, such as extent, impenetrability, motion, gravitation, divisibility, et cetera."

"That small number probably answers the views of the creator on this narrow sphere. I adore his wisdom in all his works. I see infinite variety, but everywhere proportion. Your globe is small: therefore, so are the inhabitants. You have few sensations because your matter is endued with few properties. These are the works of unerring providence. Of what color does your sun appear when accurately examined?"

"Of a yellowish white," answered the Saturnian, "and in separating one of his rays we find it contains seven colors."

"Our sun," said the Sirian, "is of a reddish hue, and we have no less than thirty-nine original colors. Among all the suns I have seen there is no sort of resemblance."

After divers questions of this nature, he asked how many substances, essentially different, they counted in the world of Saturn and understood that they numbered but thirty: such as God; space; matter; beings endowed with sense and extension; beings that have extension, sense, and reflection; thinking beings who have no extension; those that are penetrable; those that are impenetrable, and also all others. But this Saturnian philosopher was prodigiously astonished when the Sirian told him they had no less than three hundred, and that he himself had discovered three thousand more in the course of his travels. In short, after having communicated to each other what they knew, and even what they did not know, and argued during a complete revolution of the sun, they resolved to set out together on a philosophical tour of the galaxy.

THE VOYAGE OF THESE INHABITANTS OF OTHER WORLDS

Our two philosophers were ready to embark for the atmosphere of Saturn with a large provision of mathematical instruments, when the Saturnian's mistress, having got an inkling of their design, came in tears to make her protests. She was a handsome brunette, though not above six hundred and threescore fathoms high.

"Ah! cruel man," cried she, "after a courtship of fifteen hundred years, when at length I surrendered and became your wife and scarcely passed two hundred more in your embraces, to leave me like this, before the honeymoon is over, and go a rambling with a giant of another world! Go thou bean counter, devoid of tenderness and love!" She eyed Micromegas defiantly, then turned to her husband once more. "Where are you going? What do you think you are doing? Our five moons are not so inconstant, our ring not so changeable as you. But believe this, as long as you are away, I shall never love another man."

The little gentleman embraced and wept over her. Micromegas looked the other way and rose awkwardly. The lady went to console herself with more agreeable company.

Meanwhile our two scientists set out, and at one jump leaped upon the planet's ring, which they found pretty flat, according to the ingenious guess of an illustrious inhabitant of this our little earth. From thence they easily slipped from moon to moon and then a comet changing to pass, bringing with them all their servants and apparatus. They were thus carried for about one hundred and fifty million leagues, then met with the satellites of Jupiter and arrived upon the body of the planet itself, where they continued a whole year. During this time they learned some very curious secrets, which would actually have been sent to the press, were it not for fear of the pundit inquisitors, who have among them some corollaries hard of digestion.

But let's get back to our travelers. When they took leave of Jupiter, they traversed a space of about one hundred million leagues, and coasting along the planet Mars, which is well known to be five times smaller than our earth, they descried two moons subservient to that orb. Be that as it may, our gentlemen found the planet so small that they were afraid they should not find room to take a little repose, so that they pursued their journey like two travelers who despise the paltry accommodation of a village and push forward to the next market town. But the Sirian and his companion soon repented of their decision, for they journeyed a long time without finding a resting place, till at length they discerned a small speck in the distance, which was the Earth. Coming from Jupiter, they could not but be moved with compassion at the sight of this miserable spot. However, they resolved to land, lest they should be a second time disappointed. They accordingly moved toward the tail of the comet, where, finding an Aurora Borealis ready to set sail, they embarked and arrived on the northern coast of the Baltic on the fifth day of July in the year 1737.

WHAT BEFELL THEM UPON THIS OUR GLOBE

Having taken some repose and desiring to reconnoiter the narrow field in which they were, they traversed it quickly from north to south. Every step of the Sirian measured thirty thousand feet, whereas the dwarf of Saturn, whose stature did not exceed a thousand fathoms, followed at a distance out of breath. For every single stride of his companion, he was obliged to make at least twelve good steps. Imagine, if you will, a little spaniel dodging after a captain of the Prussian grenadiers.

As those strangers walked at a good pace, they compassed the globe in six and thirty hours. The sun, or rather the earth, travels the same space in the course of one day, but it must be observed that it is much easier to turn upon an axis than to walk a-foot. After having discovered that almost imperceptible sea, which is called the Mediterranean, and the other narrow pond that surrounds this mole-hill, which we call The Great Ocean, we find them returned to the spot from whence they had set out, wading through. The dwarf had never wet his mid-leg, while the other scarcely had moistened his heel. In going and coming through both hemispheres, they did all that lay in their power to discover whether or not the globe was inhabited. They stooped, they lay down, they groped in every corner, but their eyes and hands were not at all proportioned to the small beings that crawl upon this earth and, therefore, they could not find the smallest reason to suspect that we and our fellow-citizens of this globe had the honor to exist.

The dwarf, who sometimes judges too hastily, immediately concluded there were no living creatures upon earth. His chief reason was that he had seen nobody. But Micromegas, in a polite manner, straightened him out.

"My friend, with your diminutive eyes you cannot see certain stars of the fiftieth magnitude, which I easily perceive. Do you take it for granted that no such stars exist?"

"But I have groped with great care!"

The giant rolled his eyes. "Then your sense of feeling is badly lacking."

"But this globe," said the dwarf, "is ill contrived and so irregular in its form as to be quite ridiculous. The whole together looks like chaos. Observe these little rivulets; not one of them runs in a straight line. These ponds, which are neither round, square, nor oval, have any regular figure. These sharp pebbles that roughen the surface of the globe have torn the skin from my feet! Take notice of the shape of the whole, how it flattens at the poles, and turns round the sun in an awkward oblique manner so that the polar circles cannot possibly be cultivated. Truly, what makes me believe there is no inhabitant on this sphere, is a full persuasion that no sensible being would want to live in such a disagreeable place."

"So what? Perhaps the beings that inhabit it are not so displeased. To all appearance, it was not made for nothing. Everything here seems to you irregular because you fetch your comparisons from Jupiter or Saturn. That is the reason of the seeming confusion which you condemn. Haven't I told you that in the course of my travels I have always met with variety?"

The Saturnian replied to all these arguments. The dispute would have known no end if Micromegas, in the heat of the contest, had not luckily broken the string of his diamond necklace, so that the jewels fell to the ground. They consisted of small unequal karats, the largest of which weighed four hundred pounds, and the smallest fifty. The dwarf, in helping to pick them up, perceived, as they approached his eye, that every single diamond was cut in such a manner as to answer the purpose of an excellent microscope. He took up a small one, about one hundred and sixty feet in diameter, and applied it to his eye, while Micromegas chose another of two thousand five hundred feet. Though they were of excellent powers, the observers could perceive nothing by their assistance, so they were altered and adjusted. At length, the inhabitant of Saturn discerned something almost imperceptible moving between two waves in the Baltic. This was no other than a whale, which, in a dexterous manner, he caught with his little finger, and, placing it on the nail of his thumb, showed it to the Syrian, who laughed heartily at the excessive smallness peculiar to the inhabitants of this our globe. The Saturnian, by this time convinced that our world was inhabited, began to imagine we had no other animals than whales, and being a mighty debater, he forthwith set about investigating the origin and motion of this small atom, curious to know whether or not it was furnished with ideas, judgment, and free will. Micromegas was very much perplexed upon this subject. He examined the animal with the most patient attention, and the result of his inquiry was, that he could see no reason to believe a soul was lodged in such a body. The two travelers were actually inclined to think there was no such thing as mind in this our habitation, when, by the help of their microscope, they perceived something as large as a whale floating upon the surface of the sea. It is well documented that at this time an expedition of philosophers was making its return from beyond the Ultima Thule, the polar circle, where they had been making observations. The gazettes record that their vessel ran ashore on the coast of Bothnia and that they with great difficulty saved their lives. But in this world one can never dive to the bottom of things.

THE TRAVELERS CAPTURE A VESSEL

Micromegas stretched out his hand gently toward the place where the object appeared and advanced two fingers, which he instantly pulled back, for fear of being disappointed, then opening softly and shutting them all at once, he very dexterously seized the ship that contained those gentlemen and placed it on his nail, avoiding too much pressure, which might have crushed it to pieces.

"This," said the Saturnian dwarf, "is a creature very different from the former."

The Sirian placed the supposed animal in the hollow of his hand. The passengers and crew, who believed themselves thrown by a hurricane upon some rock, began to put themselves in motion. The sailors hoisted out casks of wine, then jumped after them into the hand of Micromegas. The mathematicians, having secured their quadrants, sectors, and Lapland servants, went overboard at a different place and made such a bustle in their descent that the Sirian at length felt his fingers tickled by something that seemed to move. An iron bar chanced to penetrate about a foot deep into his forefinger, and from this prick, he concluded that something had issued from the little animal he held in his hand. At first, he suspected nothing more. The microscope, that scarce rendered a whale and a ship visible, at first had no effect upon an object so imperceptible as man.

Consider that, supposing the stature of a man to be about five feet, we mortals make just such a figure upon the earth, as an animal the sixty thousandth part of a foot in height, would exhibit upon a bowl ten feet in circumference. When you reflect upon a being who could hold this whole earth in the palm of his hand and is provided with organs proportioned to those we possess, you will easily conceive that there must be a great variety of created substances. What must such beings think of those battles by which a conqueror gains a small village, to lose it again in the sequel?

The Saturnian took the microscope and made a further additional adjustment to its lens. What wonderful address must have been inherent in our Sirian philosopher when he returned it to his eye, that enabled him to perceive those atoms of which we have been speaking. When Leuwenhoek and Bartsoecker observed the first rudiments of which we are formed, they did not make such an astonishing discovery. What pleasure, therefore, was the portion of Micromegas, in observing the motion of those little machines, in examining all their pranks, and following them in all their operations! With what joy did he put his microscope into his companion's hand; with what transport did they both at once exclaim:

"I see them distinctly. Do you see them carrying burdens, lying down and rising up again?"

Their hands shook with eagerness to see and apprehension to lose such uncommon objects. The Saturnian, making a sudden transition from the most cautious distrust to the most excessive credulity, imagined he saw them engaged in their devotions and cried aloud in astonishment.

Nevertheless, he was deceived by appearances, a case all too common, whether we do or do not make use of microscopes.

WHAT HAPPENED IN THEIR INTERCOURSE WITH MEN

Micromegas, being a better observer than his traveling companion who had the gift of tongues as well, perceived distinctly that those atoms spoke. The dwarf remarked that he would not believe such a puny species could possibly communicate their ideas, for he could not hear those particles speak and therefore supposed they had no language.

"Besides, how should such imperceptible beings have the organs of speech, and what in the name of Jove can they say to one another? In order to speak, they must have something like thought, and if they think, they must surely have something equivalent to a soul. Now, to attribute anything like a soul to such an insect species appears a mere absurdity."

"But just now," replied the Sirian, "you believed they were engaged in devotional exercises. Do you think this could be done without thinking, without using some sort of language, or at least some way of making themselves understood? Or do you suppose it is more difficult to advance an argument than to engage in physical exercise? For my own part, I look upon all faculties as equally mysterious."

"I won't venture to believe or deny any longer. My mind is open and I have no opinion at all. Let us endeavor to examine these insects and reason upon them afterward."

"With all my heart," said Micromegas. The Saturnian mimicked the actions of the Sirian, who bent his head down close to the ship and its occupants. Micromegas brushed aside the hair on his forehead to expose the cerebral bump, then closed his eyes in concentration. The starmen remained motionless in this state of heightened concentration for some time until, thanks to the industry of Micromegas, the feeblest voice was conveyed into their minds. A short while later, the philosophers could distinctly discern the buzzing of the other insects that were below. In a few hours they distinguished articulate words, improving until at last they could plainly understand the French language. The dwarf understood the same, though with more difficulty.

The astonishment of our travelers increased every instant. They heard a nest of mites talk in a very sensible strain, and that unnatural enigma seemed to them inexplicable. The Sirian and his dwarf glowed with impatience to enter into conversation with such atoms. Micromegas being afraid that his voice, like thunder, would deafen and confound the mites without being understood by them, decided to communicate in the same fashion as with the Saturnian. Setting the dwarf upon his knees, and the ship and crew upon his nail, he held down his head and pretended to speak softly. Having taken these and many more precautions, he addressed himself to them in these words:

"Oh, invisible insects, whom the hand of the Creator has deigned to produce in the abyss of infinite littleness! I give praise to his goodness in that he has been pleased to disclose unto me those secrets that seemed to be impenetrable."

If ever there was such a thing as astonishment, it seized upon the people who heard this address and who could not conceive where it proceeded from. The chaplain of the ship repeated exorcisms, the sailors swore, and the philosophers invented a new philosophy, but notwithstanding all their rituals, they could not divine who the person was that spoke to them. Then the dwarf of Saturn gave them to understand what species of beings they were dealing with. He related the particulars of their voyage from Saturn, made them ac-

quainted with the rank and quality of Monsieur Micromegas, and
after having pitied their smallness, asked if they had always been
in that miserable state so near akin to annihilation, and what their
business was upon that globe which seemed to be the property of
whales. He also desired to know if they were happy in their situation, if they were inspired with souls, and asked a hundred questions
more of the like nature.

A certain mathematician on board, braver than the rest, and
shocked to hear his soul called in question, planted his quadrant,
and having taken two observations of this interlocutor, said:

"You believe then, Mr. what's your name, that because you measure from head to foot a thousand fathoms–"

"A thousand fathoms!" cried the dwarf. "Good heavens. How
should he know the height of my stature? A thousand fathoms, my
dimensions to a hair. What? Am I measured by a mite? This atom,
then, is a geometrician, and knows exactly how tall I am. I, on the
other hand, who can scarcely perceive him through a microscope,
am utterly ignorant of his extent."

"Yes, I have taken your measure," answered the mathematician,
"and will now do the same by your tall companion.

The proposal was embraced. His excellency reclined upon his
side. Had he stood upright his head would have reached too far
above the clouds. Our mathematicians planted a tall tree near him,
and then, by a series of triangles joined together, they discovered
that the object of their observation was a strapping youth, exactly
one hundred and twenty thousand royal feet in length. In consequence of this calculation, Micromegas uttered these words:

"I am now more than ever convinced that we ought to judge
nothing by its external magnitude. Oh God, who has bestowed understanding upon such seemingly contemptible substances, who can
with equal ease produce that which is infinitely small, as that which
is incredibly great. If it be possible, that among your works there

are beings still more diminutive than these, they may nevertheless, be endued with understanding superior to the intelligence of those stupendous animals I have seen in heaven, a single foot of whom is larger than this whole globe on which I have alighted."

One of the philosophers assured him that there were intelligent beings much smaller than men and recounted not only Virgil's whole fable of the bees, but also described all that Swammerdam had discovered and Reaumur dissected. In a word, he informed him that there are animals which bear the same proportion to bees that bees bear to man. The same as the Sirian himself compared to those vast beings whom he had mentioned and as those huge animals as to other substances, before whom they would appear like so many particles of dust. Micromegas proceeded in these words:

"Intelligent atoms, in whom the Supreme Being has been pleased to manifest his omniscience and power, without all doubt your joys on this earth must be pure and exquisite: for, being unencumbered with matter, and to all appearance, little else than soul, you must spend your lives in the delights of pleasure and reflection, which are the true enjoyments of a perfect spirit. True happiness I have nowhere found, but certainly here it dwells."

At this harangue all the philosophers shook their heads, and one among them more candid than his brethren, frankly owned that excepting a very small number of inhabitants who were very little esteemed by their fellows, all the rest were a parcel of knaves, fools, and miserable wretches.

"We have matter enough," said he, "to do abundance of mischief, if mischief comes from matter. And too much understanding, if evil flows from understanding. You must know, for example, that at this very moment people all over the world have divided themselves according to their beliefs and spend their days in contempt of those who believe differently, finding all manner of punishment to inflict upon the other in order to convince them to think as they do. Or else just be rid of them. Even while I am speaking, there are one hundred thousand of our own species, covered with hats, slaying an equal number of their fellow creatures who wear turbans. At least they are either slaying or being slain. This has been the case all over the earth from time immemorial."

The starman, shuddering at this information, begged to know the cause of those horrible quarrels among such a puny race and was given to understand that the subject of the dispute was a mole-hill called Palestine, no larger than his heel. Not that anyone of those millions who cut one another's throats pretends to have the least claim to the smallest particle of that clod. The question is: shall it belong to a certain person who is known by the name of Sultan, or to another whom they dignify with the appellation of King. Neither the one nor the other has seen or ever will see the pitiful corner in question, and probably none of these wretches, who so madly destroy each other, ever beheld the ruler on whose account they are so mercilessly sacrificed.

"Ah, miscreants!" cried the indignant Sirian out loud, spinning off several tornadoes in his forgetfulness. "Such excess of desperate rage is beyond conception. I have a good mind to take two or three steps and trample the whole nest of such ridiculous assassins under my feet."

"Don't give yourself the trouble," replied the philosopher. "They are industrious enough in procuring their own destruction. At the end of ten years the hundredth part of those wretches will not survive, for you must know that though they should not draw a sword in the cause they have espoused, famine, fatigue, and intemperance, would sweep almost all of them from the face of the earth. Besides, the punishment should not be inflicted upon them, but upon those sedentary and slothful barbarians who, from their palaces, give orders for murdering a million of men and then solemnly thank God for their success."

Our traveler was moved with compassion for the entire human race, in which he discovered such astonishing contrast. "Since you are of the small number of the wise," said he, "and in all likelihood do not engage yourselves in the trade of murder for hire, be so good as to tell me your occupation."

"We anatomize flies," replied the philosopher. "We measure lines, we make calculations, we agree upon two or three points which we understand, and dispute upon two or three thousand that are beyond our comprehension."

Remembering his exile from Sirius, Micromegas devised a question to ascertain the extent of the contumely on our own small globe. "How far do you reckon the distance between the great star of the constellation Gemini and that called Caniculæ?"

All of them answered with one voice: "Thirty-two degrees and a half."

"And what is the distance from hence to the moon?"

"Sixty semi-diameters of the earth." He then thought to puzzle them by asking the weight of the air, but they answered distinctly that common air is nine hundred times specifically lighter than an equal column of the lightest water, and nineteen hundred times lighter than current gold. The little dwarf of Saturn, astonished at their answers, was now tempted to believe those people sorcerers, who, but a quarter of an hour before, he would not allow were inspired with souls.

"Well," said Micromegas, "since you know so well what is without you, doubtless you are still more acquainted with that which is within. Tell me, what is the soul, and how do your ideas originate?"

Here the philosophers spoke altogether as before, but each was of a different opinion. The eldest quoted Aristotle; another pronounced the name of Descartes; a third mentioned Mallebranche; a fourth Leignitz; and a fifth Locke. The elder peripatecian, lifting up his voice, exclaimed with an air of confidence: "The soul is perfec-

tion and reason, having power to be such as it is, as Aristotle ex-
pressly declares, page 633 of the Louvrè edition:

"Εντελεχεια τις εςι, και λογος τ8 οδυναμιν εχοντϑς τοι8δι ειται."

"I am not very well versed in Greek," said the giant.

"Nor I either," replied the philosophical mite.

"Then why do you quote that same Aristotle in Greek?"

"Because it is but reasonable we should quote what we do not
comprehend in a language we do not understand."

Here the Cartesian, interposing:

"The soul," said he, "is a pure spirit or intelligence which has received before birth all the metaphysical ideas, but after that event it
is obliged to go to school and learn anew the knowledge which it
lost."

"So, it was necessary," replied the animal of eight leagues, "that
your soul should be learned before birth, in order to be so ignorant
when you have got a beard upon your chin. But what do you understand spirit to be?"

"I have no idea of it," said the philosopher. "It is supposed to be
immaterial."

"You know what matter is, at least?"

"Perfectly well. For example: stone is gray, is of a certain figure,
has three dimensions, specific weight, and divisibility."

"I want to know," said the giant, "what that object is, which, according to your observation, has a gray color, weight, and divisibility. You name a few qualities, but do you know the nature of the
thing itself?'"

"Not I, truly," answered the Cartesian.

Micromegas admitted that he also was ignorant in regard to this
subject. Then addressing himself to another sage who stood upon
his thumb, he asked, "What is the soul and what are her functions?"

"Nothing at all," replied this disciple of Mallebranche. "God made everything for my convenience. In him I see everything, by him I act. He is the universal agent, and I never meddle in his work."

"That is being a nonentity indeed." Turning to a follower of Leibnitz, the Sirian sage exclaimed: "Friend, what is your opinion of the soul?"

"In my opinion," answered this metaphysician, "the soul is the hand that points at the hour, while my body does the office of the clock, or if you please, the soul is the clock, and the body is the pointer, or again, my soul is the mirror of the universe, and my body the frame. All this is clear and incontrovertible."

A partisan of Locke chanced to be present. Asked his opinion on the same subject, he said: "I do not know by what power I think, but I know that I should never have thought without the assistance of my senses. That there are immaterial and intelligent substances I do not at all doubt. But that it is impossible for God to communicate the faculty of thinking to matter, I doubt very much. I revere the eternal power, to which it would ill become me to prescribe bounds. I affirm nothing and am contented to believe that many more things are possible than are usually thought so."

The Sirian smiled at this declaration and did not look upon the author as the least sagacious of the company. And as for the dwarf of Saturn, he would have embraced this adherent of Locke, had it not been for the extreme disproportion in their respective sizes. But unluckily there was another animalcule in a square cap, who, taking the word from all his philosophical brethren, affirmed that he knew the whole secret. He surveyed the two celestial strangers from top to toe, and maintained to their faces that their persons, their fashions, their suns and their stars, were created solely for the use of man. At this wild assertion our two travelers were seized with a fit of that uncontrollable laughter, which (according to Homer) is the portion of the immortal gods. Their bellies quivered, their shoulders rose and fell, and, during these convulsions, the vessel fell from the Sirian's nail into the Saturnian's pocket, where these worthy people searched for it a long time with great diligence. At length, having found the ship and set everything to rights again, the Sirian resumed the discourse with those diminutive mites, then promised to compose a sonnet for them and to give them a choice book of philosophy which would demonstrate the very essence of things and answer many questions by which they might benefit.

He was immediately pressed with a thousand questions, but explained that his friend, the Saturnian, had to get back home to his wife.

Accordingly, before his departure, he composed a poem for them.

The Starman's Sonnet (Author)

Shall whirling suns and dancing moons
Unto the void surrender?
The Law of Conservation cannot let their force abate:
The binding of the worlds is love most tender,
And love's lease hath no time or date.
Sometimes too quick the lathe of heaven turns,
And so, the form appears untrimmed;
Often form from form declines,
And nature's course is dimmed.
But the lumens of the stars shall not fade,
They are the light of something larger,
Whether forming or in decay.
By them we can set a course to steer by
As we sail the Milky Way.

After setting the ship back on the ocean, he made them a present of the promised book, which was addressed to the Secretary of the Academy of Sciences at Paris. Our learned crew of philosophers delivered it faithfully as requested, but after the old secretary heard their story and opened it, he saw nothing but blank paper and let out a loud guffaw.

"Ay, ay," said he, "this is just what I suspected."

Their Names Are on
Skyscrapers

Valerie Tillerson had interviewed me by phone from her home in New York City to sell her estate. Thirteen hundred acres nestled in the Blue Ridge with six houses, three barns, two lakes and a fishing cottage. She was throwing in the limousine previously owned by the Colgate family. Mrs. Tillerson turned it into a luxury resort she and her ex-husband, not unsurprisingly, had named The Tillerson. "But it got away from me when I got sick," she told me.

I should have pried deeper, but the real estate boom was over and I needed this listing. To tell the truth, I was a little nervous. I'd sold high end properties before, but never one with so much land. She said she liked the name of my company, Virginia Fine Estates, and that I handled myself well on the phone. Two hours later the listing agreement was in the mail.

The property manager, Eugene Green, was to meet me at the gates on Mountain Road. I arrived early and they were locked. I got out of my car and looked down into the valley. The spring air was clean and sweet. A gravel lane meandered down the hillside to a rustic farmhouse with an Olympic-sized pool, then climbed up steeply to a three-story chalet entangled in rose brambles. The Peaks of Otter rose in the distance above the mountaintops that ringed the valley like sleeping Titans. It overwhelmed me for a moment with its serenity. It occurred to me suddenly that the word paradise came from ancient Persia and meant a walled garden, and if there is a paradise in this world, this was it. I said to myself, How could anyone ever own this with a scrap of paper?

An old pick-up truck pulled in behind me a minute later and a leather skinned redneck in worn jeans got out.

"It's been closed for a year," Eugene said, "since she got sick. Mrs. Tillerson told me to sell the goats. They're South African. Bred them myself." He smiled. "In vitro." So much for first impressions. I had underestimated him.

There were about two hundred goats on the mountainside, and this huge white dog separated from them and trotted over to the fence. Eugene leaned over the rails and rubbed his shoulder. "This is Sam. He's a Great Pyrenees." I held out my hand for him to sniff, but he was indifferent and loped back to the herd. "He killed a coyote last winter. Over there by the edge of the pines."

"I didn't know there are coyotes around here."

Eugene kind of laughed. "Oh yeah. Big ones."

The land was divided into thirds, each with its own double gates, requiring three signs instead of one. I could see the property was unique and would need to be marketed as both residential and commercial. That would cost extra. Showing it was going to be an involved process, but that was the part I liked best. I decided to handle the showings myself. Spread among the buildings were sixty well-appointed bedrooms and fifteen suites, three dining halls, several kitchens, and a bar with a pewter counter from Provence. A half-completed cinder block health spa surrounded a second swimming pool filled with stagnant water. Someone had deep pockets, but not deep enough. You could tell when the well ran dry.

I followed Eugene to the Gilford Lodge, a racehorse stable with an outside riding ring in front. It had been redesigned as a hotel and conference center. To the side of the building was a gravel parking lot that could handle several buses. A double door entranceway with leaded glass transoms opened into a country chic lobby with a reception desk

He unclipped a keyring from his belt and rummaged for the right key. "The doors are babinga wood."

I wrote that down for the portfolio. "Do you think you could kill the weeds in the parking lot?" I asked. "I want to schedule the photographer for next week."

Eugene unlocked the door and held it open. "Sure, come on in."

I noticed the wrinkles on his face. He was at least sixty-five. The floors were coated with dust and the air smelled musty. Eugene showed me the utility room where the circuit breakers were to light the place for showings.

Two dining rooms, an upper and a lower, had a seating capacity of six hundred. We stood beside a grand piano in the downstairs dining area and looked out over the sea of tables. "You must have had quite a staff to serve so many people," I said. "How many employees worked here?"

He chewed his lip and nodded. "About thirty. And a chef for a while."

"I'll need any journals or books you have to show buyers the profitability and operating costs. What kind of income did you generate?"

"Mrs. Tillerson has the records up in New York. You better ask her." He indicated to follow him down the hall. "Let me show you the bar." In a tavern-like room with a walk-in fireplace, next to a pewter covered bar, was a stuffed coyote mounted on a stand. "That can't be a coyote," I said.

Eugene grinned. "Eighty pounds. I shot it out by the chalet. Mrs. Tillerson had it stuffed to add to the ambience."

"It's huge." I studied the curling lips on the snout. The taxidermist had captured the perfect snarl.

He showed me the rest of the property, which took six hours. At the end of the day we returned to The Gilford and flipped the circuit breakers off. We left through the front lobby and locked the door. The Gilford was the soul of The Tillerson, and it had to look good.

"Can you get someone to clean the floors? They're pretty dusty."

He looked at me sadly. "Nobody around here will come. It's just me. I still got to bush hog, fix the roof, paint the shutters, and weed whack five miles of fence. And kill the weeds in the parking lot. Between you and me, I don't know what I'll do if this place doesn't sell. I haven't been paid for six months."

I exhaled slowly. "Why do you stay on, Eugene? Why don't you quit?"

"If I quit, I won't get my back pay. Besides, I got more than just that invested in this place."

"Is that why the locals won't come?"

"She owes everybody around here money."

I looked at the sun setting on the Peaks of Otter and thought about my commission. I let out a sigh. "I'll come back tomorrow and take care of it. Hell, I'll buff up the tables, too. A little shineola never hurts."

She said she wanted thirteen million, but she would take ten and agreed to a six percent commission. I was stoked up to get started. My marketing team put it in three different MLSs and took out ads in *The Wall Street Journal* and several luxury property magazines.

Immediately there were interested parties, though the price was high. The first was a couple who wanted to turn it into an orphanage. The husband owned a media company and told me, before I even asked, that he was selling off some TV stations. He seemed to have the means to make the purchase. They fell in love with the place on the initial showing and came back a few days later for another. After I had given them the second full tour, Mrs. Tillerson came down from New York City and we all met together in the office of The Gilford. The wife was deeply committed to their mission and broke into tears after explaining they wanted to make an offer for the sake of the children.

"How many children?" I asked.

She pulled a Kleenex from her purse and blew her nose. "About twenty girls in the beginning. We'll finish the spa and teach them to be beauticians." I glanced nervously at Valerie. She knew how to wear a poker face.

"Many institutions receive grants from benefactors," said her husband. "Perhaps Mrs. Tillerson could finance us, and we could pay her back over a ten-year term." The meeting ended quickly.

After the orphanage couple, I showed The Tillerson to a builder, then two days later to someone who wanted to turn it into a wedding resort. They were interested but the price was out of their reach and she wasn't willing to come down on hers. Then I got a call from a Larry Williams. He had found the property on-line and looked at the on-line portfolio. We spoke for twenty minutes and he explained he wanted to start a business college that taught Objectivist principles. He had to drive up from North Carolina, so the next afternoon would work best for him to see it.

When selling high end property, I try to eliminate curiosity seekers and the financially unqualified. A background check revealed little more than that he taught at NCU. His name was mentioned on an Ayn Rand blog as a contributor to an objectivist publication. Replies to his commentary often ended in, be selfish,

Larry. *Was he a little fish in a big pool?* Real Estate would be a great business if it wasn't for the customers.

He was tall with unkempt rust colored hair and asked a lot of questions about who was on the county board of supervisors. After I took him through, I could tell he was interested. The bones were there to start a small college and board three hundred students. It actually made sense. I asked him if he had investors he was working with.

He glared at me angrily. "I have backers and I want you to show it to them. Can you be here next Wednesday morning?"

"Absolutely." I tried to pick his brain. "If they're coming a long way, I'm sure I can have Mrs. Tillerson let them stay in The Gilford. The view of the valley from there is beautiful."

"That's a great idea."

"Let me know who is coming and I'll have the rooms made up for them. Could you email me their names? Mrs. Tillerson will need to register them."

I felt his hackles rising. He could tell where I was going. "I can't give them to you without their permission. You already know their names, they're on skyscrapers."

I tried not to laugh. "Like John Galt?"

He didn't think it was funny.

On Wednesday Larry arrived with his wife and daughter in a Jaguar sedan. His wife was a beautiful woman half his age. His daughter was a quiet girl of twelve years. Eugene pulled up in his pickup and I introduced him and myself to them. Larry started walking to The Gilford without saying hello. I looked in the Jaguar and it was empty. "Larry, where are your backers?" I shouted after him.

"They want to come Monday," he said without stopping. He pulled on the lobby door and turned to face us, shrugging his shoulders.

"It's locked. Hold on," I said, running over with Eugene at my heels. Larry's daughter stood behind him as Eugene fumbled for the keys. When the lock clicked, Larry yanked the door open. It slammed into her head and she stumbled backward.

"Jesus, she's going to have a lump!" his wife cried.

Larry stood there frowning. "She'll be okay."

"I'll get some ice," said Eugene. He returned a few moments later with a bowl of ice from the downstairs kitchen. I wrapped a couple of cubes in a towel from the restaurant linen closet and handed it to Mrs. Williams. She sat down beside her daughter on the couch by the registration desk and held it on her forehead. I felt sorry for both of them. Her daughter hadn't said a word.

Larry went ahead by himself to the upstairs dining room. Eugene and I followed a minute later and stopped in the doorway. Larry was sitting on a table rubbing his ass back and forth across the top. He looked at us and hopped back to the floor.

"He's stamping it with his scent," I whispered to Eugene.

Eugene's eyebrows raised an inch. "Never seen nothing like that."

"Neither have I, but I know when somebody wants to buy." I gave Eugene a shoulder bump. "He's going to make an offer."

I got a call from Larry on Monday morning. The backers couldn't make it, but he was still working on it. I had doubts I would ever hear from him again.

That afternoon a real estate developer named Lou Gibrarri phoned me from DC. He wanted to see the property Wednesday. I did background checking and got a warm feeling right away. Gibrarri had sold a shopping center in northern Virginia the week before for eight million dollars. He was also wanted for tax evasion on land he owned in Richmond. According to *The Times Dispatch*, Gibrarri was the most delinquent taxpayer in Virginia. It was hard to guess the profit he made on the sale, but if it was substantial, he would want to avoid taxes by burying it in The Tillerson. The modus operandi fit.

He was supposed to meet me by the gates overlooking the valley. On a gorgeous day the view melted them, that's why I wanted to start there. But he didn't show up. Cell phones don't work well in the valley, so I drove up the hill to the chalet and called his office from there. His secretary explained the weather in DC was bad. He was flying to Lynchburg on his own jet and the pilot said no go. He would be there two o'clock. That sort of thing comes with the territory.

Lou Gibrarri arrived at three in the afternoon, just when I lost all hope and decided to leave. He got out of the rental car with two mesomorphs who looked like bodyguards. They all wore sunglasses. His were silver, like the guard with the rifle in *Cool Hand Luke*. I saw myself extending my hand in the reflection.

"I'm really sorry," said Lou. "I know how I feel when someone keeps me waiting. My pilot wouldn't take off until noon. These are my lawyers, Bill Harris and Gerry Knave." They stood clasping their wrists and nodded.

"Don't worry about it," I said, smiling. I handed them each a portfolio of the property. I knew Lou was taking the view in. "It usually takes about six hours to see everything. We can start at the chalet…"

"I don't have that much time." He rifled through the portfolio and stabbed at The Gilford Lodge. "I got an hour and a half. Show me The Gilford, and this." He stabbed The Homestead House, a reconstruction of a southern plantation with hexi-columniation and monitor windows on the roof. The mansion overlooked a fifteen-acre spring fed body of water called Hamilton Lake.

I drove them over to The Gilford. The lodge had an upstairs and a downstairs kitchen. You could tell he loved the stainless. Lou's lawyers followed us at a polite distance as I took him through. He looked over the lower dining area and stared at the crystal chandeliers, then stood on his toes and flicked the prisms. When we toured the bedrooms, I pointed out the views of the peaceful bush hogged hills. On the way out, I took them through the bar. He stopped at the coyote and held up his hand and turned around slowly, shaking his head.

I gave him a big grin. "What do you think?"

He took off his glasses and I wished he hadn't. Someone I knew told me Lou was in the mob. I believed it. The eyes were dead and gray, shark-like. You could bury a lot of bodies on thirteen hundred acres. "The five Ws," he said.

"Five Ws?"

"Yeah. You got to know the five Ws. Who, what, when, where. So, why? All that money she spent. I know who, what, when and where. But why is she selling it?"

Those eyes had seen too much. I looked away at the bar to escape his gaze. "She was sick. It got to be too much for her."

Gerry Knave stroked his nose and tilted his head sideways with a cracking sound. Lou was still holding his sunglasses when I faced him again. "Can I see a profit and loss statement?"

"Her accountant is in New York. Can you give me a day or two?"

He frowned at his watch and put his sunglasses back on. We toured Homestead House, then walked toward Hamilton Lake. On the way was a barn. "What's in there?" he asked.

"A garage. There's a limo that comes with the estate."

He wanted to see it. One side of the barn was used to garage a limousine. "Mrs. Tillerson bought it from William Colgate, the toothpaste tycoon." I rolled back the door, revealing a Mercedes 600 Long Wheelbase Landaulet with opposing rear seats covered by a convertible top. Some considered it to be the finest Mercedes ever made. The black finish glistened beneath the dust. "They used it to pick up guests from the airport."

The lawyers walked around the car speaking in low tones. Lou motioned to me to come outside with him. We stepped into the sunlight. "Can you do a 1031 tax exchange?"

"The forms are in my briefcase."

"I'll do eight million with a 1031 exchange."

Low, but he might come up. Legal, and he was good for it. "I'll write up the offer," I said, beaming.

"Just a verbal. See what she says."

I called her home in New York City. The phone rang several times before the maid picked up. The line hissed and popped. "She's out of town. She didn't say when she's coming back."

Valerie Tillerson didn't return my emails or phone calls. And neither did her ex-husband, whom she had instructed me never to call. At first, I actually believed she really was sick, then I came to accept the fact that something was going on. But we were incommunicado. I was sure Lou didn't believe me when I told him I tried many times to get hold of her to present his offer. After that, his secretary always said he was in a meeting. I got the picture.

Then, after four days, as though nothing had happened, Valerie called to let me know she had met with Larry Williams in New York privately. Her own lawyers had drawn up the sales contract without me.

I tried to sound calm, not knowing whether to be furious at her or happy for her that it was sold. "What did you agree to?"

"Fifteen million. Including the furnishings. But don't worry, you're going to handle everything for me. I overnighted the contract. You should get it today."

"Well ... good going. I'm dying to know, who are the backers he keeps talking about?"

"He never told me who they were." I thought the line dropped for a moment, but she was still there. "He's going to build a golf course community with townhouses to finance the college."

I had to hold my phone with both hands to keep from dropping it. "This is no-money-down creative financing at its worst. Valerie, townhouses in a rural area will require total rezoning to high density. They won't go for it. Even if they did, it could take two years to get it through and that's how he's going to pay you."

"I'll wait."

Another one of life's lessons. If there was to be a settlement, it was a long way off. I'd have to wait, too.

A townhall was held in the Faber Building to determine how the local people felt about a college with townhouses. The chairman read a summary of Larry Williams's proposal, then invited questions. Larry sat hunched over in the front row wearing a Brooks Brothers suit and a pinched smile. People's feelings were mixed. They asked questions about taxes going up, traffic, and where the townhouses would go. He was dismissive and skirted their questions, puffing up the jobs that would be created. My doubts grew as the sweat stains expanded from beneath the arms of his jacket.

The board wanted architectural plans and more information on the proposal, including the number of students and their housing requirements. They needed proof of the license to operate an educational institution and a list of faculty names.

A second meeting was scheduled in two months. When the townhall adjourned a reporter tapped me on the shoulder. "Could I talk to you outside?"

Her name was Ann Porter and she wanted photos from the portfolio to do a feature story on Valerie Tillerson and the history of the Tillerson. It dawned on me this was a good way to promote the idea to the community and to repair the poor public image Larry Williams had created for himself.

The Sunday paper ran a special on the Tillerson; a column on the front page and two pages with color photos in the Living section. I called Ann to let her know what a great article it was.

"Thanks very much," she said, "and thanks for those photos. They added a nice touch. By the way, I want to ask you something."

"Anything you want."

"A neighbor of Mrs. Tillerson told me they used to have cockfights in one of the barns. Do you know anything about cockfighting over there?"

"Everything was first class as far as I know. Cockfighting? No." But by the time I had driven half a mile down the road I has a nasty feeling it was more than possible.

Getting to the settlement table is an involved process for a large estate. The sale was contingent upon a successful inspection and that meant considerable effort was needed to ensure things were in good working order. Eugene and I spent two days making a list of needed repairs. Bad flashing on the roof of the chalet had caused stains on a bedroom ceiling. I found a dead bat in one of the showers. The roof and siding needed power washing and the brambles had to be cut down.

"We got to clean this up, Eugene. I don't want a case of buyer's remorse ruining the deal." I smoothed over the covers on one of the beds. "Why aren't the beds made?"

"I had to make them myself after things went downhill."

"What about the staff? What were they getting paid for?"

Eugene plumped up a pillow and tossed it onto the bed. "That's just it. They weren't getting paid."

"Did they have cockfights in one of the barns?"

He fiddled with his ear, frowning. "Maybe, but how would I know?"

Loyalty to your client comes with the territory. I would handle it for Valerie. I made a mental note: *Clean up feathers in the back of the barn by the Homestead House.*

Larry Williams came through with the license and a list of six possible faculty members, but the courses would be taught online. During the following weeks he contacted me several times to admit surveyors onto the grounds. When the plans for development were submitted to the board of supervisors, they set the final vote for approval to March 31st. On the morning before the vote he called me. He told me he needed to be let on the property to see Hamilton Lake.

I waited at the main gates until quarter past ten. A mix of disappointing snow and freezing rain was coating the roads. The trees rattled with ice. I found his name in my contact list and phoned. "Larry, I'm at the gates. How far away are you?" The connection was so bad I couldn't understand him.

He came storming through ten minutes later and slid to a stop, then motioned me on. I drove past Homestead House and led him down the hill to the lake. I got out first and extended my hand to shake as he stepped out of his car, but he lost his footing and grabbed the car door instead.

"Watch out, it's getting slick," I said.

"I'm fine. Let's go down by the pier."

Larry led the way to the edge of the lake by the entrance to the pier. He pointed with his finger, shaking it for emphasis. "Do you see over there?"

I sighted down his finger to the other side of the lake. "The fishing cottage?"

He faced me and jabbed the finger into my chest. "Right. Well, she's taking the cottage and ten acres."

I knew he was up to something again. "That's reserved. It's in the contract."

"It's not in your marketing portfolio and that's an egregious misrepresentation. I'm suing your ass!"

The sound of a car starting came from across the lake. A sedan emerged from behind the fishing cottage.

"Who the hell is that?" said Larry.

"It looks like Valerie Tillerson's car. She must have come down for the vote tomorrow." The wheels whined on a patch of ice, then caught traction in the gravel.

"You didn't tell me she was here."

"I didn't have any idea."

We continued arguing as she made her way to the fishing pier. She parked her car next to mine. "Hello, gentlemen. What's going on?"

I took a deep breath to explain. "Mr. Williams has just told me he will sue me because I didn't mention in the portfolio that you are keeping the fishing cottage."

"And ten acres. Don't forget about that."

Valerie motioned us to follow her. "Let's go out on the pier where we can get a better look. Larry, you and I signed the contract with the part about the cottage and ten acres."

"It's slick. Be careful, Valerie," I said.

The pier extended thirty yards out over the lake. We followed her to the empty boat dock at the end. "The ten acres is for a drive-

way to the main road from the cottage. It's going to be my little retirement getaway. It doesn't interfere with any of your plans, Larry."

I gave him a reassuring smile. "You and Valerie put that in the
contract in New York. I wasn't there."

He stepped on my foot and stuck his face in mine. I couldn't step
back. "I've got too much at stake in this." He tapped on my chest
while he thought of more insults. "You're incompetent and unpro-
fessional. I'm already talking to my lawyer."

I tried to extricate my foot from beneath his wingtip, but he
leaned closer and pressed harder. All the intimidation was about
something else. He was trying to maneuver me into position, but I
couldn't tell what he was after.

"What do you really want, Williams?" I stared at his bulbous
nose which somehow began to look like an undernourished turnip.

"I'm bringing in my own broker and you're going to assign your
commissions to them. And I want the keys to everything, right
now. I can't have you waste my contractors' time while they wait
around for you to let them in. I'm on a tight schedule."

"The keys are turned over at settlement," I said, "that's how it
works."

"Stop it boys," said Valerie.

"What good are keys when *you* don't have any backers,
Williams. How are you going to start building without backers?
Now take your fucking foot off mine!"

I don't remember punching his nose, but it was bleeding. Valerie
tried to pry us apart and shoved Larry. The loss of control was apparent on his face as both his feet slid off the pier. His forehead contacted the edge with a wooden thud. The water was over his head
and the skim of ice didn't slow his plunge. His momentum drove
him farther out. A large flap of skin had peeled from his forehead,
but with surprisingly little bleeding.

"God, that's got to be cold, Larry," I said. He didn't reply.

His camelhair coat opened and floated up around him, then the corners started sinking. You could see the label on the inner pocket: Saks Fifth Avenue. Valerie crouched down at the edge. "You never had a pot to piss in, you bastard."

"I'll get the life preserver," I said.

She put her hand on my arm. "I will." She stood slowly and felt her way carefully over the black ice to where the preserver hung on a nearby post. It was difficult for her to release the ring, her hands were shaking so badly. There were only a few thin lines of coagulated blood floating in the water when she got back. She threw it over the spot where he went down.

The wintery mix turned to flakes of white snow, blending the frozen surface of the lake into the hills. We watched together as the hole in the ice filled with slush.

I looked at Valerie. "Should I call the police? It was an accident – right?"

She had stopped shaking. She looked back at me and tilted her head at a dangerous angle. "I suppose you are right."

"You know, I tried to tell you. Now we're back to square one."

She laughed wistfully. "I'm used to waiting."

My phone said NO SERVICE. I had to drive to higher ground. On the way out I closed the gates behind me and took in the mountains ringing the valley. The walls of paradise were still standing. I felt lighter. At peace. My own kind of selfish. Waiting won't be so hard.

Breaking Them with
Words

Sofia had just fallen back to sleep when she heard the gunshot. At first she thought she had dreamed a gun firing. She groped her way downstairs in the near dark. Feeling reassured no one was in the house, she entered the garage and turned on the light. Ari was slumped against the wall, sitting on a stack of Helsinki Times she had tied into a bundle, an advancing line of red spreading slowly over the headlines dated 18 September, 1952: Zarja Sets Sail for Russia to Pay Off Last of 300 Million. In his hand was his service pistol.

The funeral was held on Wednesday afternoon. They had picked a plot out together at the church cemetery, but the pastor said sorry, but no, suicide was a sin. Sofia took it up with the bishop; he agreed with the pastor. A military funeral at Hietaniemi Cemetery was granted. The chaplain was non-denominational and told her such things were not to be judged by men, and he would perform a full service.

The burial consisted of a small gathering of Ari's and her families and an American wearing a camel hair coat and a Homburg hat. A gun salute and bugle sounded the end of the service, and seemingly on signal, it began to rain.

Her mother rubbed her shoulder and told her she and her father would be waiting in the car. Sofia remained at the end of the grave, feeling and unthinking. After a few minutes, she felt a light touch on her arm.

"Mrs. Salonen, I'm Jack Williams. I managed the IBM project for him at the bank."

She recognized the name. "He had spoken of you highly. I hope you don't judge him too harshly."

"He was a deep thinker, a good man. It must be hard for you."

"Thank you."

"I have something of his you should have. I have to go back to the States tomorrow, so I thought I should give it to you now." He handed her a manila envelope.

"What is it?"

"It's a story he wrote. He wanted to have it published and asked me to help him with the grammar, but you know, his English was excellent."

"He never mentioned it to me. Thank you, Mr. Williams."

He handed her his card. "Call me Jack." He offered his arm and they walked back to the road.

"Why don't you stay with us tonight?" her father asked as she climbed in the car.

Sofia shook her head.

Ari had handled their financial matters, collecting the records and bills in his desk in the study, always paying them early. As the bills started to accumulate, Sofia began going through them. In one of the drawers was a stack of correspondence. As she examined the letters she came across one with a return address from Salla. It was a personal thank you for a loan to refinance a hotel. The last few lines caught her attention: I had the piano rebuilt, and the remodeling of the hotel came out better than I had hoped. The basement is a bistro with a wine cellar now. You and your wife must come to visit. I'll always remember your kindness. Your loving friend, Verá. Sofia went to the living room and sat at the piano, playing the first few measures of the Appassionata too slowly. It was Ari's favorite piece, but she never could get it right. She poured herself a drink and sipped slowly, looking over the shelves filled with busts of composers and Hellenic vases they had collected over the years. They both loved music and history. She loved his sensitivity. Sometimes he would hide the tears in his eyes when he was moved by a passage of music, and she would pretend she didn't notice.

Sinking down on the sofa, she picked up the envelope Jack Wilson had given her from the coffee table. She opened the flap, sliding out the manuscript Ari had been working on, neatly double spaced with wide margins.

IN THE MIDDLE OF NOWHERE

I had served in the Finnish Jaeger Brigade during The Winter War in June of 1941, transferring to the 6th Division in July 1944, as a major. The advancement was more due to my language skills than fighting skills; I speak English, Russian, German, Swedish and Finnish. They decided to send me to Salla in eastern Lapland near the Salpa Line where a liaison was needed to coordinate operations with the German Mountain Corps.

When I arrived, it was held by the Soviets on the eastern fringes. Finland's resources had become depleted from the struggle against Russia, and we allied with Germany, hoping to quickly gain our lands back. Stalin threw everything into the fight, knowing Moscow was Hitler's next stop via Finland.

The locals had been evacuated, but among the few remaining was a woman named Verá who ran the hotel on the edge of town near Lake Märkäjärvi. Salla had been a popular tourist spot that advertised itself as the middle of nowhere, but the war had put an end to tourism. Verá's hotel was used as quarters for both Finnish and German officers and the rest of the soldiers were given temporary barracks just outside town. Some of the billets were trenches with log and earthen roofs, hard to spot from a distance.

My duties were to brief our new allies on the techniques of Arctic warfare and facilitate communication between the officers of the two armies. We made some inroads against the communists, but British naval blockades and a constant influx of Russian equipment and troops pressed us to hold on to our gains.

On an unusually hot day in August, I returned to the hotel from a briefing at headquarters. As I walked through the lobby, a German major sat in a battered leather chair next to the piano, pulling sheet music from under the bench lid.

"Wie gehts? Ari Salonen," I said.

He extended his hand. "Jon Ehler. I think we will be working together."

We shook as the other officers began filing into the dining room. "Let's get something to eat, before it's too late," I said. We found two empty places at the end of a crowded table. I yelled across the room: "Verá, go to the basement and bring up a bottle of cognac off the top shelf for my friend and me."

"Why don't you come down and help me pick out something good? You can reach on top better than me."

"We might be down there all night."

Verá laughed defiantly. "The longer the better." It was a little flirty banter we all played to take our minds off things; she enjoyed it as much as the men. Her husband was killed when he ran into the Soviets while picking up supplies. The staff had fled when the town was evacuated, so she had to serve the officers single-handedly. She was the only woman left in Salla.

She reappeared with a bottle and two glasses. "Don't you two make trouble, I've got my hands full already."

I poured and nodded with a Kippis to my German counterpart. Jon was finely chiseled and handsome, looking too young to be a major, yet not having the superior air many Nazi officers had. We drained our glasses.

"Everything tastes good with cognac," I said.

"Or with butter," said Jon. "When's the last time we've had any of that? So, you have a wife and family?" He held the glass in his palm with the stem between his fingers, warming the cognac with his hand and sniffing.

"I'm engaged. Her name is Heleena. She's going to get her degree in history, then we'll get married. How about you?"

"Pianos are my passion. My family has been building pianos for generations. At first I thought I wanted to do something else, so I got a job designing elevators, but I couldn't stand it. Then I went to work at Rönisch Piano in Dresden. Before the war I was designing a self-playing piano that plays the violin and cello sections. How about another?"

"Good idea," I said, and poured. "That's incredible, I've never heard of such a thing. When this is over you can go back and finish your work."

"There will be nothing but rubble by then. What are you going to do?"

"I have a degree in economics; I'll get a job in a bank. With a little luck, we may end up with a nice house and kids, and maybe a summer place on the beach."

"That sounds nice." He emptied his glass.

An SS captain leaned over and tapped Jon on the shoulder. "Play something before you're too drunk."

"The piano is out of tune."

He continued tapping. "Come on, play."

Jon raised the lid before sitting at the bench. Composing himself briefly, he began the first few notes of the Appassionata, feeling out the tired wippens and jacks of the old grand, adjusting himself to its eccentricities and worn spots, then filled the lobby with waves of music, taking us up and out of the battered hotel and away from the tasteless food and tiredness. His large hands were ten kings, coaxing the soul from the piano with long, slim fingers. We sailed above the war on the wings of Ludwig Von Beethoven, suspended in mother of pearl twilight. It wasn't the cognac. When he ended, I fell back into the lobby, wondering, how could someone like Jon, with such a gift, end up in a shithole like this?

He had won me. There was a time when he could have played anywhere in Europe if he had the desire. In the days that followed, he would pull out sheet music from the piano bench and his orderly, who had an excellent voice, would accompany him, and so I became his prisoner.

One evening, as we sat in the lobby, he asked, "Major, where is your orderly? I haven't seen him."

"Killed. Hardly eighteen. They haven't been able to spare anyone to replace him."

"I'll send over one of ours. His name is Walter Unrau and he's a skilled batman."

"You're generous. I've been borrowing the other officers' orderlies and they're growing tired of it."

Corporal Unrau was very personable and efficient. He had things ready before I asked and seldom needed drawn out instructions. I came to rely on him a lot.

As the war dragged on it became apparent things were going wrong. Due to bad intelligence, Hitler underestimated the Soviets' ability to build new armies. Fresh communist forces slowed the advance to Moscow until the winter set in, bogging them down with snow and frostbite.

Reports in German, Finnish, Russian, and English were sent to headquarters in an unending stream. News of the German offensive falling apart came in, warning of a darker outcome for Finland.

As August wore on to September, I received word that we were beginning talks with Zhdanov in Moscow. An armistice between Finland and the U.S.S.R. would be signed within a week, putting an end to our collaboration with Germany.

I had returned to my room late one evening. Corporal Unrau always checked in on me to see if I needed anything or had orders for the next day, but it was late. I knocked on his door and poked my head inside. He jumped up from his cot and snapped to attention looking pale. His eyes were swollen.

I'd seen the look before. "Everything okay, corporal?"

"My brother was killed in action. His destroyer went down."

The look on his face was the loneliest I had ever seen. I embraced him and patted his back.

"I apologize, sir. I'm the last one. My family is gone."

"The uniform can't protect us from these things. There's no reason to."

I wanted to get him off the front, but he was under German command. "You must stay alive," I said to him. "I'd send you away to a typing pool, but it's not up to me. I'll ask for you. When things are better, maybe they'll send you to Berlin."

The next morning there was a clean uniform in the closet. I picked up my papers from the desk, neatly arranged and clipped together, then went down to the dining room and found Jon.

Verá came to take my breakfast order. The officer across the table was pounding his fist on the table, ranting: "No butter, no juice, no toast."

She frowned at him sternly. "Stop your whining."

"There are worse things that can happen," I said.

"Worse than no butter?" asked Jon, cracking the top off his egg and getting yolk everywhere.

"You could be Walter Unrau—he lost his brother and his family. We have to get him out of here."

He dabbed at the yolk with his napkin, making the mess worse. "We break them down with words and put them back together with words. We command them with orders to do our bidding, unspeakable things beyond description. When we ask why God, God is struck dumb by our folly. It would be better if musicians ran the world, then none of this shit would happen. I'll say something at headquarters. It may take a few days."

There was a light still burning inside him. Verá came to take my order. "What will it be today, Ari?" she asked.

"Just coffee."

"You seem very glum. How about eggs and ham? Get off to a good start."

"No."

Jon scooped away the inside of the egg with his spoon. "He's in a quiet mood, Verá."

She moved on to the next table.

"You're right," I said to Jon. "Musicians should run the world. There is something else we need to talk about, but not here, it's too crowded. There's something in the wind."

"More bad news?"

"We need to meet somewhere private. Did you ever have a real Finnish sauna—a savusauna?"

Jon raised an eyebrow. "I don't think so."

"The stones are heated by a wood fire without a chimney. The smoke fills the room, then when the fire dies the smoke is let out. The stones stay hot for hours. There's one by the lake, I'll have them get it ready. We can drive out before dinner."

"I will go only on condition that I will be beaten by an old woman with a stick."

I hadn't laughed in a long time. "If I can't find one, I will beat you myself."

The sauna was forty yards from the shoreline. The smoke had cleared, leaving a clean scent of maple and birch in the dark interior. We undressed and went in.

"Some prefer to jump in the lake to cool off, but one time I was bitten by mosquitoes so badly I decided to use the shower from then on," I said.

He looked at me disapprovingly. "Is that why you're always scratching your ass?"

I threw some water on the stones and we sat down. "I didn't invite you to talk about mosquitos. We have been meeting with the Soviets and will sign an armistice that will end our alliance. We must turn over all Germans. Or shoot you if you don't cooperate."

"We've fought together side by side. Could that happen?"

"I don't know, we're caught in the middle." The water stopped its hissing as it dissipated.

"What about you? Would you?" He began rubbing his forehead mechanically.

"I give you my word I'll do everything in my power to help you and your men escape."

"When is this to happen?"

"In two days."

Jon wiped the sweat from his brow and slid to the lower bench. "We could do it under cover of darkness."

"There's a problem; they want prisoners. The Russians are five kilometers to the east and they'll be watching. We must make it look good. If you put your men in the underground billets, we can come in from the south and fire into the ground as they escape. That might fool them long enough for you to get to the north to rejoin your forces."

He leaned back on his elbow, frowning. "And I have your word your men won't hit us?"

"We'll only shoot to miss," I said, "you have my word."

"And the other officers—they will all cooperate?"

I nodded.

Jon let out a sigh. "You are a good man, Ari, I mean it."

At headquarters, I explained my plan to the other officers and they agreed. I turned in early that night. After I fell asleep there was a knock on the door. I forced myself awake and opened it to find Verá standing there in the hall. The weather had been getting cooler, yet she was wearing a thin summer nightgown that let the light from the hallway pass through around her body. I sometimes wondered if our playful words about the basement were a little more than just words.

"What is it, Verá?"

"I need to know exactly what's going on. There's a rumor going around the Russians are taking Salla back."

"Don't worry, the Russians will need a good hotel to stay in. When I see their commanding officer I'll tell him you'll be serving his head on a platter if he isn't respectful."

She shook her head. "I can't stay. Not after what they did to my husband."

"I can get you a letter of safe conduct. Is there someplace you can go?"

"My family is in Niesi."

"I'll have it for you tomorrow."

"Ari, what will happen to you, will you be leaving?" Verá stepped closer.

"They'll keep me for a couple of days, then send me off somewhere, I suppose."

She threw her arms around me. "Thank you, Ari."

I cannot say I wasn't tempted, but the moment passed and we separated as friends.

The next morning I was informed the Russians were sending a small contingent of Allied Commission observers ahead of their troops. I contacted Jon and informed him they would have to move out immediately. The timing was not good now, but the plan could still work. We moved into position near Lake Märkäjärvi and began firing as soon as they began to leave. To fool the Russians, reports were issued that there were casualties but they managed to escape.

When I returned to headquarters that afternoon, I was told by the aide-de-camp Soviet officers were waiting to see me. They were congregated in the hall.

I saluted. "I'm Major Salonen."

"Poltzin," said a haggard-looking colonel, without returning the salute. He looked up from the report and eyed me rudely. "Where are they?"

"I'm afraid they got away. They knew we were coming."

"Do you think we're idiots?"

"Colonel, there was no way to keep anything from them."

"Go after them. If you can't capture them, kill them."

"We don't have the trucks or tanks to pursue. The few we had, you took away. Those are your terms in the treaty."

Poltzin stared in a cold rage. "There will be severe reprisal if you don't capture or kill all Germans, no matter how you do it. Those are the terms you agreed to. All Nazis will be captured or killed."

His face was nearly touching mine, the eyes dead and gray, as though covered by a third lid, like a shark's haw.

"Is that clear, Major?"

"Yes, Colonel, I understand."

"These are your new orders, effective immediately," said Poltzin.

I took the dossier he waved under my chin, then saluted. After reading through them, I had Verá's safe conduct letter drawn up and stamped, then headed back to the hotel and slipped it under her door. As I walked out the lobby door to return to headquarters, a truck driven by Walter Unrau pulled up. Jon got out carrying a leather satchel.

"What the hell are you doing, get out of here," I said.

"I forgot something."

"The Soviets are here. Get out now."

He ran inside, returning in a moment with the bag bursting full of sheet music. Halfway to the truck it split open, spilling music on the ground. As he snatched up a handful of sheets, Poltzin came running down the street with his revolver drawn, leading a dozen of my men.

"They're escaping, shoot!"

Jon jumped into the truck. "It's no use, it's too late," I shouted through the window.

He motioned to go forward. "Remember your promise."

"We have orders to shoot for God's sake!"

He nodded to Walter and the truck lurched forward.

Poltzin aimed from across the street, but couldn't get a clear shot. "Salonen," he shouted. The men looked at me, waiting.

"Ammuskella!" I said.

The barrage sounded like one shot and the horn went off. Jon fell out and stumbled to the ground, landing face down, his coat tattered with holes. I ran to him, kneeling down beside him. He was groaning deeply and making a rattling sound, trying to raise himself while still holding the music in his good hand. The other was a mangled pulp, slipping in the blood.

I unbuckled my pistol and held it to the back of his head. I had never killed once myself in all my time in the service, only by the orders I had given. When I pulled the trigger and felt the life go out of him, so did my own. I have been his prisoner ever since, reliving that day every day, in the middle of nowhere.

* * *

Sofia shuffled the pages together and stuffed the story back in the envelope. Weeks grew into months and she came to blame herself. He wasn't the same when he came back, but she thought that was just something wars did. She thought of herself as a good listener, but she must have missed something. He had never talked about any of it; the story he had written was the only attempt he had made. She told herself it was only a story.

The house reminded her of Ari and she needed to get out. Sofia accepted her parents' invitation to spend Christmas with them. During Christmas Eve dinner, her father suggested she do some traveling, then she remembered the letter from Verá.

The day after Christmas she returned home and got the hotel address from the envelope. Uncertain if she was ready to confront the ghosts of the past, she made the reservations anyway. It was fourteen and a half hours to the railway station at Kemijärvi, then an hour and a half by bus to the town of Salla. The bus let her off on Savukoskentie Street near Verá's hotel, the Borea. It was three in the afternoon and the town was lit by street lamps and Christmas decorations.

The Borea was rustic with square cut logs painted red and balconies with views of the water. The interior had a new feel to it. It had been remodeled in a Scandinavian design of whitewoods and grays with wooden ceilings. On one side of the foyer was the dining room, on the other, the lobby with a grand piano. A life size Yule goat stood next to the desk by the door. Sofia tapped the bell gently, wondering if she might be greeted by Verá.

"Moi," said a college-aged girl, appearing from a door behind the desk.

"I'm looking for Verá Pedarson."

"What is this in reference to, may I ask?"

Sofia smiled. "I'm not selling anything. I have a reservation. Would you tell her Sofia Salonen is asking for her?"

The girl spoke on the phone, and a moment later, a tall athletic looking woman walked to the desk. "You must be Sofia," she said cheerfully, "I'm glad you decided to come." She looked about the empty foyer. "Where is Ari?"

"He passed away recently. It's just me."

"Oh no. I'm very sorry." Her eyes began to tear.

"I wasn't sure I should come," said Sofia. "I should have written back, I'm sorry."

Verá shook her head. "You mustn't apologize. Let's sit in the lobby where we can talk." They found seats near the piano. "I saw him less than a year ago when I came to the bank to sign the loan papers. He seemed healthy then."

"He shot himself in the temple with his service revolver." The piano loomed in the silence. "It was on the day after the war debt was paid to Russia."

Verá turned away. "Something happened here."

"That is why I came to Salla. I want to know."

"Ari had a German friend, an officer named Jon Ehler, who was different than the others. He was a gifted musician and used to play on this piano. He didn't believe in the war any longer, and neither did Ari. When the armistice was signed, Ehler and an orderly named Unrau tried to escape, and Ari was ordered to have them shot. He had to use his own pistol on Ehler." She let out a deep sigh.

"It's true," said Sofia.

"What is true?"

"Something Ari had written. Thank you, Verá."

When Sofia got to her room, the first thing she did was open the balcony doors and look out over the frozen expanse of Lake Märkäjärvi. The Lapp sky had taken on a deep blue. Along the horizon on the far side, the clouds were tinged serenely with nacre. After a few minutes the deep cold penetrated into her pores and she backed into her room and closed the doors.

Sofia spent several days exploring the villages nearby and went on a cross country skiing expedition along the Salpa defense line. She found the earth-covered billets where the soldiers stayed, and the Sotka cellar where four Finns had defended themselves against Russian grenades. They were the only reminders of the war she could find. Everything was freshly painted and inviting. The war debt had been paid, settled by the bankers and accountants. Reconstruction had hidden the scars, but she was not finished healing.

On the morning of her return to Helsinki, she sat down to breakfast with Verá. "I'm coming back. I was looking for something and I think I found it."

"What is that?" asked Verá, cracking the top off her egg.

"There is no museum here. I have a purpose now; I'm going to build a war museum. Will you help me? Ari left me some money—I know he would want it."

Verá soaked up the yolk with her toast. "I will do all I can. I promise."

"Breaking Them with Words" has previously appeared in *The Scarlet Leaf Review* and *Everywhere Stories, Volume III.*

www.ingramcontent.com/pod-product-compliance
Lightning Source LLC
Chambersburg PA
CBHW070612120726
47909CB00004B/1191